Jacqueline Wilson

CHRISTMAS CRACKER

HAVE YOU READ THEM ALL?

LAUGH OUT LOUD
WE ARE THE BEAKER GIRLS
MY MUM TRACY BEAKER
THE STORY OF TRACY BEAKER
I DARE YOU, TRACY BEAKER
STARRING TRACY BEAKER
THE WORST THING ABOUT MY SISTER
DOUBLE ACT
FOUR CHILDREN AND IT
THE BED AND BREAKFAST STAR

HISTORICAL HEROES
HETTY FEATHER
HETTY FEATHER'S CHRISTMAS
SAPPHIRE BATTERSEA
EMERALD STAR
DIAMOND
LITTLE STARS
CLOVER MOON
ROSE RIVERS
WAVE ME GOODBYE
OPAL PLUMSTEAD
QUEENIE
DANCING THE CHARLESTON

LIFE LESSONS
THE BUTTERFLY CLUB
THE SUITCASE KID
KATY
BAD GIRLS
LITTLE DARLINGS
CLEAN BREAK

RENT A BRIDESMAID
CANDYFLOSS
THE LOTTIE PROJECT
THE LONGEST WHALE SONG
COOKIE
JACKY DAYDREAM
PAWS & WHISKERS

FAMILY DRAMAS
THE ILLUSTRATED MUM
MY SISTER JODIE
DIAMOND GIRLS
DUSTBIN BABY
VICKY ANGEL
SECRETS
MIDNIGHT
LOLA ROSE
LILY ALONE
MY SECRET DIARY

PLENTY OF MISCHIEF
SLEEPOVERS
THE WORRY WEBSITE
BEST FRIENDS
GLUBBSLYME
THE CAT MUMMY
LIZZIE ZIPMOUTH
THE MUM-MINDER
CLIFFHANGER
BURIED ALIVE!

FOR OLDER READERS
GIRLS IN LOVE
GIRLS UNDER PRESSURE
GIRLS OUT LATE
GIRLS IN TEARS
KISS
LOVE LESSONS

✮ ABOUT THE AUTHOR ✮

Jacqueline Wilson is one of Britain's bestselling authors, with more than 35 million books sold in the UK alone. She has been honoured with many prizes for her work, including the Guardian Children's Fiction Award and the Children's Book of the Year. Jacqueline is a former Children's Laureate, a professor of children's literature, and in 2008 she was appointed a Dame for services to children's literacy.

Visit Jacqueline's fantastic website at www.jacquelinewilson.co.uk

Jacqueline Wilson

Illustrated by Nick Sharratt

CHRISTMAS CRACKER

CORGI YEARLING

CORGI YEARLING

UK | USA | Canada | Ireland | Australia
India | New Zealand | South Africa

Corgi Yearling is part of the Penguin Random House group of companies
whose addresses can be found at global.penguinrandomhouse.com.

www.penguin.co.uk
www.puffin.co.uk
www.ladybird.co.uk

First published 2014
This edition published 2015
Reissued 2019

006

Printed and bound in Great Britain by Clays Ltd, Elcograf S.p.A.

A CIP catalogue record for this book is available from the British Library

ISBN: 978-0-440-87120-0

All correspondence to:
Corgi Yearling
Penguin Random House Children's
80 Strand, London WC2R 0RL

* CONTENTS *

TRACY BEAKER'S CHRISTMAS

My name is Tracy Beaker. I am writing this in my private secret journal. (I snaffled it from the school stationery cupboard – don't tell!) No one's allowed to read it on pain of death. This especially means you, Justine-Nosy-Littlewood! If I catch you peeking I'll bash your big nosey-nose so hard it will pop out the other side of your head.

I can't stick Justine. She's the worst girl ever in the Dumping Ground, and she's been totally unbearable today, showing off because this teensy little parcel arrived for her in a small jiffy bag. She wanted to open it straight away, but Jenny saw the sticker on the back: *Do not open till 25th December!*

'Oh wow!' Justine cried. 'I bet it's my Christmas present from my dad! I knew he wouldn't forget me. See, Tracy Beaker! My dad's sent me a special present. What about your precious mum? *She* hasn't sent you a parcel yet, has she?'

'I'm expecting an extremely large parcel to arrive any day soon,' I said. 'My mum always buys me *fabulous* presents. Not titchy little rubbish presents like that one from your dad. I bet it's just something boring like a pack of chewing gum, or – or a squashed up pair of socks.'

'I think it's exactly the size of that fantastic iPod I saw in a magazine. I wrote and told my dad all about it. I bet it's that iPod!'

'Dream on, you loser,' I said, but my heart was starting to thump painfully. Maybe Justine's dad really was giving her an iPod. Some of the other kids in the Dumping Ground had already been sent presents from their families. Mike and Jenny were sorting them all in a special cupboard. It was nearly full now. Well, they'd have to keep all the remaining space for a great big present from my mum. Something even better than an iPod. Maybe my very own drum kit? An enormous flat screen television to put on the wall of my bedroom? A mega-fancy silver twenty-two gear bike? *All three???*

I waited so hopefully for the post van to arrive the next day. And the next. And the next. I got soooo excited when the postie staggered up to the door of the Dumping Ground with a great big box on Christmas Eve – but it wasn't for me, it was for my ex-best friend Louise.

'Oh, fantastic! That's my auntie's handwriting!' she said, shaking the box happily.

'Don't get too worked up – it's ever so light. It's probably one of those trick presents. It's a great big box but you'll find there's just some tiny weeny worthless present inside, like a packet of paperclips, or – or a pack of three knickers,' I said.

'No, I think it's light because it's probably clothes. My auntie's dead cool. I bet it's fantastic designer T-shirts or a little sparkly top and leggings,' said Louise, rushing off to tell Justine.

They are best friends now. I don't care in the slightest. They're welcome to each other.

'*I'm* your friend now, Tracy,' said weedy Peter, and he tried to cosy up to me. I pushed him away sharpish.

'I am Tracy Beaker. I don't need friends,' I said. 'Especially silly little squirts like you.'

I hoped he would stomp off, but he just stayed by

my side, patting my shoulders, almost like he was *pitying* me.

'I understand, Tracy,' he said. 'You're in a mood because you're sad your mum has forgotten to send you a Christmas present.'

'No, I'm not!' I said, giving him a push. Though actually I was. And I felt mean when weedy Peter toppled over backwards. It was only a *little* push too. Jenny came running when she saw him sprawling on the floor and asked what had happened.

'Did you push Peter, Tracy?' she said fiercely.

'Oh no, Tracy didn't push me,' Peter insisted. 'I just tripped.'

I felt meaner than ever. I followed Jenny back to her office. I eyed up her bulging cupboard full of presents. I felt a little watery eyed, although of course I didn't cry. I'm tough Tracy, I never ever cry.

'Am I the only kid here who doesn't have a Christmas present?' I mumbled.

'Well, Peter hasn't got any presents either,' said Jenny.

'Oh,' I said.

'But maybe Father Christmas will come and give you both presents,' said Jenny.

'Look, I'm not a little kid. Whoever believes in Father Christmas?' I said. 'Jenny – can *I* give Peter a Christmas present?'

Jenny smiled at me. 'I think that's a lovely idea, Tracy.'

'But I haven't exactly got any pocket money left. So what shall I do? Shall I try and make him something?'

Jenny thought. 'You like writing a lot, Tracy. Why don't you write him a little poem? I'll give you a special piece of paper and you can do little pictures all round the margin.'

So I sat in privacy in Jenny's office and created a surprise Christmas poem for Peter. It wasn't very long:

Happy Christmas Pete,
Sorry I knocked you off your feet,
I think you're quite sweet!

It was the thought that counted, after all. I gave it a border of holly and crackers and reindeer and Christmas trees and coloured them all in very carefully, and then added *Love from Tracy xxx*

'I think Peter will love his present,' said Jenny.

And he really did! Father Christmas came to him in the middle of the night and left him some truly cool presents – a computer game and a wrist watch and a torch and a giant box of chocolates – but guess which present he said he liked best!

'I love my special Christmas poem, Tracy!' he said, his eyes shining. 'It's my best present ever.'

I might revise my ideas about Father Christmas, because he left me great presents too. He gave me sparkly Converse boots and a big paintbox and my very own mobile phone – and a new notebook for my secret journal with a *lock and key*.

I'm writing in my new journal now, so ya boo, sucks to you, Justine, you can't read a word of this! I don't care that you've taken Louise away from me now. I've got my new best friend Peter instead.

* WRITE YOUR OWN *
CHRISTMAS POEM!

A special poem, rhyme or limerick would make a
lovely present for a friend or someone in your family.
You could tuck it under the wrapping paper of a bigger
gift, or sneak it into a stocking on Christmas morning!
Here are some handy Christmas words to inspire you.
Lots of them rhyme or have very similar sounds,
which is a good place to start when writing a poem!

Snow • Glow • Ho ho ho • Bright • Night • Tonight
Light • Berry • Very • Merry • Present • Gift
Surprise • Robin • Reindeer • Carrot • Cake
Carol • Santa • Sleigh • Snowman • Stocking
Star • Bell • Tinkle • Twinkle • Glitter • Winter

Find a piece of paper and write yours!

DAD'S NEW JOB

'**W**hy can't I have an iPad for Christmas, Mum?' I asked. Again. 'Nearly everyone else in my class has got one. Well, not a proper big iPad – a mini one. OK, it doesn't have to be an actual iPad. You can get much cheaper tablets. One of them will do. Go on, say yes!'

'Give it a rest, Livvy,' said Mum, kicking off her shoes and putting her feet up on the sofa. She started massaging her toes. 'My feet aren't half killing me.'

'Tickle toes, tickle toes!' my little brother Dexter cried, running to tickle her.

'Give over, Dexter!' Mum squealed, trying to bat him off, but she couldn't help laughing.

This was great. I needed her to be in a good mood.

'Go on, Mum, say yes. All I want from Father Christmas is one little measly mini tablet,' I wheedled.

'I don't think Father Christmas will be coming to visit us this year,' said Mum. 'He wrote and told me. He's very sorry and he'll try to pop over next year. Times are hard in Lapland too.'

'Oh, ha ha. Sometimes I wonder if Father Christmas is just pretend,' I said.

'What?' said Dexter, stopping tickling and staring at me open-mouthed.

'Shh, Livvy. Don't you dare spoil things for Dexter!' Mum said crossly. 'Take no notice of Livvy, Dex. She's just in a mood.'

I felt a bit mean. My little brother Dexter can be a bit of a pain at times, but he's a game little kid. He believes everything you say, which I suppose isn't surprising seeing as he's only four and three quarters, still one of the babies in reception in the Infants at school. Whereas I'm in the Juniors now and I've got a lot of things sussed out.

I'm pretty sure there's no such person as the Tooth Fairy. I even have my doubts about the Easter Bunny. I couldn't quite make up my mind about Father Christmas. If he was real I hoped he *would* come. He couldn't leave me without any Christmas presents at all, could he? And if he couldn't manage an iPad mini, couldn't Mum and Dad save up for one?

All right, I know they hadn't got much money this year, not since Dad lost his job. We used to have HEAPS of money. We had a new car and a new kitchen and Dexter and I had great clothes and loads of lovely presents. But then Dad's company got taken over just before Christmas last year and the new people didn't need him to work for them any more.

'Don't you worry,' said Dad. 'I'll get another job in a matter of weeks, you'll see.'

My dad's always right. But he wasn't right this time. He didn't get a new job in weeks and weeks. He didn't get a new job in months and months. He's tried to get countless office jobs but no one seems to want him. He was fine for a bit but now he just lies on the sofa watching television and he can be really grumpy at times. Even with Dexter, and everyone loves him because he's so sweet.

'You mustn't mind Dad too much. He's feeling pretty miserable,' said Mum.

She still had her job as a receptionist but she didn't earn much money. We couldn't go away on holiday this year. We lost our new car. We can't have stylish new clothes any more. Some of the nastier girls in my class sneer at me because I wear cheapo trainers now and my clothes aren't designer, they've just got supermarket labels.

I don't really care too much. I have two best friends, Angel and Sarah, and they don't ever say anything horrid about me. But they've both got iPad minis now. Oh, I so want my own.

'I know we haven't got much money but I'm sure we could cut down on food a bit. I'd be very happy to go without boring old vegetables and I'm not even that keen on fruit,' I said. 'And who wants meat and fish? I'd love to have a big plate of chips for supper every night and I bet Dexter would like that too. See! We could save heaps of money that way.'

'You need to have proper balanced meals to stay healthy,' said Mum. 'Now stop being so lippy, Livvy.'

'Lippy Livvy, lippy Livvy!' Dexter chortled.

'Why can't Dad stop being so hopeless and get any old job anyway?' I said.

'What?' said Dad.

He'd been so quiet lying on the sofa I thought he was asleep. I could have bitten off my tongue. I hadn't really meant to say that. I loved my dad to bits and I didn't think he was hopeless at all. I felt really bad now, especially when I saw Mum's expression.

'Sorry, Dad,' I said quickly.

'No, you're right, Livvy,' Dad said sadly. 'It's time I gave up hoping I'll ever get to be an office manager again. It's time I really did take any old job.' He got slowly off the sofa and started leafing through the local paper.

'Don't take any notice of Livvy. She's driving me nuts banging on and on about this wretched mini iPad,' said Mum.

'Well, it's not such a crime to want a decent Christmas present, is it?' said Dad, circling one of the adverts. 'There! I'll go after this job tomorrow.'

Mum had a look.

'What? Don't be so daft! Look, you've got a degree in business studies, you're highly qualified, you had twenty staff under you in your old job,' Mum said. 'I'm sure there'll be a good office vacancy soon, maybe early in the new year.'

'Well, if there is then that will be fine. But meanwhile it's time I pulled my weight.' Dad ruffled my hair. 'Thanks for shocking me into action, Liv.'

I still felt bad. I'd have sooner Dad had been cross with me. I decided I'd better stop going on and on about an iPad mini, even though I wanted one so much. I was pretty sure Dad wouldn't get this job, whatever it was.

But he did. He picked up Dexter and me from school and took us to the swings on the way home. He even bought us a whippy ice cream, and we hadn't had one of those for ages.

'We're celebrating my getting a new job,' he said.

'Great way to celebrate, Dad!' I said, licking away.

Dexter agreed. His ice cream was looking horribly slobbery and he'd spilled it all down his coat, but he was looking very happy.

'Congratulations, Dad,' I said. 'So what sort of job is it then?'

'Oh, it's just a job job,' said Dad. 'Still. There were heaps of guys there applying. I had to do a long interview so they could see I've got the right qualities. And I got it! It's only temporary, but it's a start, eh?'

Mum was also very vague about Dad's new job.

'Good luck, darling,' she said. 'I do hope it goes well.'

'What are you going to be doing, Dad?' I asked.

'Oh, this and that,' said Dad.

I couldn't understand the great mystery. I discussed it with Angel and Sarah. Their dads both had jobs. Angel's dad was a bus driver. Sarah's dad was a nurse in a hospital. So was her mum.

'Do you think my dad's got a job as a bus driver or a nurse?' I asked.

'I don't think he can be a bus driver because he'd have to leave really early in the morning to get to work,' said Angel.

'My mum and dad go to work early too when they're both on their day shift,' said Sarah. 'But you have to do a lot of training first if you want to be a nurse.'

'You've got to learn to drive a bus if you're going to be a bus driver. Obviously,' said Angel.

'Well, if he's not a bus driver or a nurse, what is he then?' I asked.

'Ask him, silly!' said Sarah.

'I have asked him! He just won't say,' I said.

'Maybe he's doing a job he's a bit ashamed of?' said Angel.

'Like what?' I said.

'Perhaps he's been recruited as a spy!' said Angel. She watches a lot of adventure films.

'My dad's not like flipping James Bond!' I said.

'Maybe he's been recruited by a gang of criminals!' said Sarah. She watches those films too.

I don't think they were really being serious. They were just winding me up.

'He doesn't work the right sort of hours to be a spy or a criminal,' I said. 'He leaves the house the same time as Mum and Dexter and me, and he gets back about six.'

'That's office hours,' said Angel.

'Yes, but he hasn't got an office job, he couldn't get one.'

'Maybe he's working in a shop?' Sarah suggested.

'I wish!' I said. 'The Apple shop! Wouldn't that be cool! Then he could get me a discount on an iPad mini!'

When Dad came home on the Monday after his first day in his mysterious new job he looked tired out.

'How did it go, love?' Mum asked.

Dad pulled a funny face. 'Well, it was pretty exhausting – but in a good way,' he said.

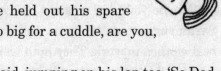

He picked up Dexter and gave him a cuddle. Then he held out his spare arm. 'You're not too big for a cuddle, are you, Livvy?'

'Course not!' I said, jumping on his lap too. 'So Dad, have you been doing lots of selling?'

'My job doesn't involve any kind of selling,' said Dad.

'So what *does* it involve?' I said.

Dad gently took hold of my nose and pretended to twist it off.

'You don't give up, do you, Miss Nosy!'

'Quit pestering your dad, Livvy,' said Mum. 'Come and help me stir the sauce for supper.'

'Dad always makes the sauce,' I said. 'It's his speciality.' My dad was great at cooking, especially when we ate Italian.

'Yes, but he's had a really busy day,' said Mum.

'Hey, has Dad been cooking then? Is this new job of his in a restaurant? Oh, is it a Jamie's?' I asked, getting excited.

'No, it's not a Jamie's or any other restaurant. Now do give it a rest, Livvy.'

I couldn't. I looked carefully at my dad, trying to suss things out. He went to his mysterious work in the same old jumper and trousers day after day, but in his old job he'd worn a smart suit and liked to wear different shirts and fancy ties.

'Maybe your dad wears a uniform for his new job?' Sarah suggested. 'My mum and dad never wear their best clothes to work. They both wear blue uniforms.'

I tried to imagine my dad in a uniform.

Then I heard Dad asking Mum to take his old work trousers to the cleaners for him.

'This little kid spilled his can of coke all over me!' said Dad, laughing ruefully.

So Dad worked amongst children.

'Perhaps he works in a McDonalds?' Angel suggested.

'He said he doesn't work in any kind of restaurant,' I said.

'Do you think he could be a lollipop man?' Sarah asked. 'You know, taking little kids across the road. They have to wear a white coat as a uniform.'

Ah! I thought I'd guessed right now. But when I casually said, 'How was the traffic today, Dad?' he just looked at me and laughed.

'No traffic! Now give it a rest, little Miss Sherlock!'

'But *why* won't you tell me, Dad?'

'I don't want to, isn't that reason enough? Now quit

pestering me or your chances of getting that iPad mini for Christmas are nil,' said Dad.

I shut up mega fast immediately! It was lovely that we had a bit more money now. Mum started buying a few things for Christmas when we went shopping on Saturday. She bought a box of posh chocolates and a Yule log and wine for her and Dad and fizzy lemonade for Dexter and me.

'Hurray!' we said, because we hadn't had special chocolates or fancy cake or nice drinks for ages.

'Can we do some Christmas present shopping too, Mum?' I asked. 'I need to buy something for Angel and Sarah. And you and Dad and Dexter.'

'All right then. So long as you don't take all day,' said Mum.

'Can we go to Mitchells' Christmas Bazaar?' I said.

Mitchells was the big department store in the shopping centre. It always had a huge selection of cheapo stuff for children without much pocket money doing their Christmas shopping – i.e. *me!* Mum always loves going to Mitchells too, so I was surprised when she pulled a face.

'I think you might find just as good things in the Arcade or the Pound Shop,' she said.

'Oh, Mum! Go on! Let's go to Mitchells.' I gave Dexter's arm a little tug. 'You want to go and see the dancing teddies at Mitchells, don't you, Dexter?'

This was dead crafty. Dexter simply adores the animatronic teddy bears in the Mitchells' entrance hall. He is always transfixed with delight and dances about too, singing all their silly songs.

'Yeah, I love the teddies! Let's go and see them *now*,' he said, clapping his hands.

Like I said, Dexter is so sweet that no one can ever resist him, not even Mum.

'Come on then,' she said, sighing.

We spent ages watching the teddies. Dexter danced and sang. Don't laugh, but I danced and sang a little bit too. I used to like those teddies just as much as Dexter when I was little.

Then we got to go to the Christmas Bazaar in the basement and I rushed round all the counters choosing my presents. I made Mum and Dexter wait outside because I didn't want them to see what I was buying. I bought a pink glass bangle for Angel and a blue glass bangle for Sarah. I very badly wanted a glass bangle for myself, pink or blue or any other colour, but I didn't have any money left after I'd bought a tiny yellow teddy for Dexter, some rosy soap for Mum and a pen for Dad. I minded a bit, but it couldn't be helped.

'All sorted?' said Mum, smiling at my carrier bag of

presents. 'Let's go home then, before the shops close. We don't want to spend ages waiting at the bus stop.'

Just then there was a loud announcement on the store's intercom.

'Last chance today to see Father Christmas in his grotto! Make your way now to the second floor!'

'Father Christmas!' Dexter squealed. 'Oh, let's go and see Father Christmas!'

'No, darling, we have to get home,' said Mum.

'But we need to meet Father Christmas to ask him to come and see us!' Dexter insisted. 'You said he wouldn't come to us this year, Mum. We have to see him now!'

'Oh Dexter, don't make a fuss! Don't worry about Father Christmas. I think he probably will be able to come to see us this year after all,' said Mum.

'Oh, please please please can we go and see him, just to make sure?' said Dexter.

'No we can't, so stop making a silly fuss, Dexter,' said Mum.

Dexter stood where he was, his little face agonized. Big fat tears started dripping down his cheeks. He didn't say another word. He didn't need to.

'Oh dear, stop crying. All right, we'll pay Father Christmas a very quick visit,' said Mum.

We hurried up to the second floor and joined the queue to pay to go into the grotto.

'It's mostly for little kids, Dexter's age or even younger. You don't really want to go too, do you, Livvy?' said Mum.

'Yes!' I said, knowing that you always got a present when you went to see Father Christmas in Mitchells. Maybe he'd give me a glass bangle!

'I could find a nice lady in the café over there to keep an eye on you while I pop in with Dexter,' said Mum. 'I'll buy you a strawberry milkshake.'

I loved strawberry milkshakes. I'd drunk gallons of them back in the days when we had lots of money. But I thought I'd like a glass bangle even more. And I didn't want to be left out.

'Why can Dexter go to see Father Christmas and not me?' I said. I wasn't as good at crying as Dexter, but I made my eyes go all watery. 'Do you like Dexter better than me?'

'Oh, stop it. I love you both the same, you know that. All right, all right, you can see Father Christmas too, if you really must,' said Mum.

She sounded very anxious. Perhaps she didn't have enough money left for two tickets? We waited in the queue for ages. I began to wonder if I'd made the right decision. I could have been sitting in comfort with a strawberry milkshake rather than shuffling endlessly through Father Christmas's boring grotto, with little whiny kids all around me.

Dexter wasn't whiny. He was deliriously happy, singing 'We're going to see Father Christmas soon soon soon,' again and again. And again. It started to get almost as annoying as the other kids' whining. But then at long last we shuffled round a corner and there was a strange lady dressed in a red and green costume.

'Hello, I'm Father Christmas's special little elf friend,' she said. 'And who have we here?'

'I'm Dexter and this is Livvy,' said Dexter. 'Is Father Christmas really here? Mummy said he might not be able to come this year.'

'Oh dear,' said Mum, looking embarrassed.

'Father Christmas is right here and he wants to meet you now,' said the elf, and she took us both by the hand and led us round the next corner, Mum following.

There was Father Christmas just as promised, wearing his familiar red outfit and big boots, his white beard hanging down his chest. He looked very surprised to see us. I felt a bit shy and silly but Dexter went leaping forward.

'Hello, Father Christmas! I'm Dexter and I'm so so so glad you're here! Will you come and leave us a present on Christmas Eve, even if it's just a little one? I promise I've been a good boy. Well, I've been *quite* good, haven't I, Livvy?'

'Dexter's been very very good,' I said truthfully. I took a deep breath. 'I haven't always been very good myself, because I so want an iPad mini and I've nagged about it, but if you could possibly spare me one I'll be ever so grateful.'

'I'll do my best, but I can't make any promises,' said Father Christmas.

He spoke in a funny deep voice, as if he was pretending to be older than he really was. His face didn't look old at all, in spite of his long white beard. He had a lovely smiley face, a bit like my dad.

Then I looked a little closer. I stared and stared, my mouth open. It *was* my dad! Oh my goodness, Dad was Father Christmas! *This was his new mysterious job!*

'I know who you are!' I blurted out.

Mum's hand clamped down on my shoulder. 'Father Christmas' shook his head at me, nodding at Dexter. I suddenly understood. Dexter was little enough to believe wholeheartedly in Father Christmas. Mum and Dad had kept quiet because they didn't want to spoil it for him.

'I know who you are too!' Dexter cried.

Oh no, had he guessed after all?

'You're Father Christmas, that's who you are,' said Dexter, laughing.

'Ho ho ho, that's absolutely right, little boy,' said 'Father Christmas', obviously greatly relieved. 'Now, what might you like for Christmas?'

'I'll have just a little present, I don't mind what, but can you bring an iPad mini for Livvy, because she wants one ever so much? And she might let me play games on it too,' Dexter said earnestly.

'Oh Dexter!' I said, feeling absolutely overwhelmed. I wanted to scoop him up and hug him.

'Father Christmas' looked quite moist-eyed too.

'You're a grand little chap,' he said. 'I'll do my best.

Meanwhile I've got a little present just for today for both of you.' He delved in his sack and brought out a big blue parcel for Dexter and a pink one for me. The pink one was small and flat. Just the right size for a glass bangle!

'Thank you, Father Christmas!' I said enthusiastically.

'Thank you, Father Christmas,' Dexter echoed.

Another Christmas elf led us outside.

'I love Father Christmas,' Dexter declared, ripping the paper off his present. 'Oh wow, look, a toy truck! I can take all my animals for a ride in it.'

Dexter fancies himself as a mini farmer and tends a small plastic herd of three cows, one sheep and a chicken, keeping them in small pens in a shoe box.

I opened my pink present carefully. I so so so hoped it would be a glass bangle. It wasn't. It was a little doll in dungarees.

'I'm way too old for dolls,' I said disgustedly. 'I would have thought Father Christmas might have realized this.'

Mum frowned.

'I'm not sure Father Christmas always chooses the presents in his sack,' she said, flashing me a warning look.

'I think it's a lovely dolly,' said Dexter. 'If you don't want her, Livvy, I'll have her as my farmer wife. She'll be very helpful milking the cows when I'm busy.'

So Dexter ended up with two presents and still had a full belief in Father Christmas. Whereas I now realized what I'd started to suspect. Father Christmas wasn't real at all. He was just someone's dad dressed up in a silly costume.

I couldn't wait to get to school the next day to tell Sarah and Angel.

'Don't you dare!' said Mum. 'They might be very happy still believing in Father Christmas. You don't want to spoil it for them.'

'Oh per-lease, Mum! Look, I haven't believed properly for ages,' I said, fibbing a little bit.

But when Dad came home he also said I mustn't tell anyone.

'Thank you for not spilling the beans to Dexter, Livvy. You mustn't dream of telling anyone else either. Promise?'

'All right,' I sighed, though I thought Angel and Sarah and I would have a right old giggle if I told them about Dad's new job.

I couldn't help bringing up the topic of Father Christmas at school the next day.

'Guess what, my mum took me to see Father Christmas at Mitchells along with Dexter and all the little kids,' I said.

I waited for them to roll their eyes or sneer, but they simply looked interested.

'I haven't been to see Father Christmas yet,' said Angel. 'Did you tell him you'd like a mini iPad?'

'I told Father Christmas last year I wanted a giant teddy almost as big as me – and it was there waiting for me when I woke up on Christmas morning,' said Sarah.

Goodness, it looked as if my friends were still true believers, just like Dexter! There was a little bit of me that wanted to tease them and tell them the truth – but I knew that would be unkind. So I kept quiet, even though it was a bit of a struggle.

I gave them their Christmas presents from me on the last day of term. They both *loved* their bangles. Angel gave me a Jenna Williams paperback and Sarah gave me a stationery set. It was very kind of both of them but I would have much sooner had a glass bangle.

Dad was working hard all day every day until late on Christmas Eve. He came home looking exhausted but happy.

'I actually got given a bonus for covering for one of the other chaps,' said Dad.

He was muttering this quietly to Mum while I helped Dexter concoct paper Christmas presents for his farm animals.

'So did you manage to get the you-know-whats?' Mum whispered.

I was so excited that I couldn't help peering over at them. They saw and immediately changed the subject.

Dad started saying that he'd really enjoyed this new job, and once Christmas was over he was going to be much more adventurous in his job-seeking, and prepared to try his hand at anything.

I was very happy for Dad – but I longed to know if he'd really managed to buy me an iPad mini from his Father Christmas wages.

I had to wait for Christmas morning to find out. There was a very promising small square parcel waiting at the end of the bed with a label that read 'With love from "Father" Christmas.'

It was my very own longed-for iPad mini! I was so so so happy! I went running into Dexter's room and he was crowing excitedly too.

'Look what Father Christmas has brought me!' he exclaimed, showing me a proper toy farmhouse. 'Oh, my animals are going moo and baa and cluck because they're so happy! And look what I got in my Santa stocking too – more animals for my farm, a donkey and a turkey and three little piglets!'

'Oh, my stocking! I didn't check it,' I said running back to my own bedroom.

I'd tipped my stocking onto my bedroom carpet by accident. There were the usual sweets and chocolate and little orange – and five carefully wrapped presents, all the same size. I tore the paper off excitedly. I found one two three four five glass bangles, pink, purple, red, blue and green! I slipped them all on my arm and they clinked and jingled together wondrously.

I hadn't breathed a word to Mum or Dad about longing for a glass bangle. Now I had five! I think there is a real magic Father Christmas after all!

* HO HO HO! *

Try these Christmas jokes out on your class or your family!

What do you get if you cross Father Christmas with a duck?
A Christmas quacker!

What do Father Christmas's little helpers learn at school?
The elf-abet!

What do snowmen wear on their heads?
Ice-caps!

What do angry mice send each other at Christmas?
Cross mouse cards!

What happened to the girl who ate Christmas decorations?
She got tinselitis!

Why are Christmas trees so bad at sewing?
They always drop their needles!

What's red and white, red and white, red and white?
Father Christmas rolling down a hill!

GARNET'S RETURN

I can't wait to see her! She's been gone for so long. We've never even spent a day apart before, and yet now we've been separated for three whole months! It's been such rubbish without her.

I'm talking about my twin sister, Garnet. We're identical. Well, we don't really look identical now, because I've given myself a radical new haircut. I was sick of those stupid plaits. No one ever used to be able to tell us apart, which was a huge bonus when it came to confusing and exasperating people at school. That's my speciality, confusing and exasperating. I can do it easy-peasy without even thinking.

I'm the naughty twin, Ruby. I'm also the eldest and the fastest and the noisiest and the bossiest. I used

to think I was the cleverest, but when Garnet and I
sat this stupid exam to get into a girls' boarding school,
Marnock Heights, we both got a shock. Garnet passed
the exam and I didn't. Of course, I didn't really try too
hard. And I didn't actually want to go to boarding school
anyway. It sounds horribly boring and strict and stuffy.
Yes, I'm sure I'd absolutely hate it if I went there.

Garnet says she actually likes it. This is amazing,
because my sister is so shy and scared she generally
can't do anything without me. I was sure she'd cry
floods of tears and come rushing back home in a week
or two. But she's stuck it out and all her postcards and
emails say she's having a great time. This is too weird.
I'm sure she's just trying to stop me worrying about
her. She must be so lonely without me.

*I go home tomorrow! I absolutely can't
wait! It's been such ages since I've seen
Ruby. Of course we write all the time.
Well, I write. Ruby doesn't always
bother to email me back straight
away. I had to ask her to stop sending
postcards because everyone reads them
and sometimes she says very rude
things. She even does rude drawings.
They're funny, of course, but they're not
at all the sort of stuff you'd want the*

teachers to see. I showed my best friend Lucy one of Ruby's jokey cards. I thought she'd roar with laughter but she just looked a bit puzzled.

'It's a bit infantile, isn't it?' she said.

Infantile is one of the worst things you can say about anyone at Marnock Heights. All the girls in the older classes are always saying it about us.

I got upset and went off by myself and cried a bit. I know it's extremely infantile, but I'm a terrible cry-baby. Lucy came to find me and put her arm around me and said she was very sorry and didn't mean to upset me.

'I didn't say you were infantile, Garnet. I'd never say that, even if you were, because you're my best ever friend. I just said it about your sister,' she said.

'I know – but we're twins, you see, and if you say something bad about Ruby it's like you're saying it about me too,' I said. 'You don't understand because you haven't got a sister, let alone a twin.'

'Mmm,' said Lucy. 'But if you don't mind me saying, from the emails I've seen she sounds a very bossy twin. She's always telling you you're stupid or hopeless or pathetic.'

'Yes, but that's Ruby's way. She doesn't really mean it,' I said.

'Mmm,' Lucy said again.

I decided not to argue further. It's not Lucy's fault.

 41

And she is my best friend. Though of course Ruby is my bestest best friend. Oh, I can't wait to see her!

We're going to take the car to Hineford to meet Garnet from the station, Dad and Rose and me. Rose is our stepmother. We used to hate her but actually she's not such a bad old stick when you get to know her. Of course, she'll never take the place of our lovely special mum – but I'm not going to write about her or I'll start crying.

We lived with Dad and Gran till Rose came along, but now we've moved to this bookshop in the country – and Gran's gone to live in sheltered housing. She says she likes it there. She's got this friend called Albert. I suppose he's Gran's boyfriend, which is seriously embarrassing. Rose has invited him to come for Christmas. That's going to be weird. But at least Garnet will be back and it will be sooooo brilliant.

Oh-oh. Christmas. I haven't gone out and bought my presents yet, and I spent all my money on a new game for my Xbox. Oh well. I'm sure Garnet will have presents for everyone, and then I can just add *Love from Ruby*.

I'm writing this on the train, on my way home! It was sad saying goodbye to everyone at school. I even felt a bit teary saying goodbye to the teachers! I gave Jamilla a big hug – and she seemed delighted with the scarf I'd knitted her. It was worse saying goodbye to Lucy. We share a rabbit in the school zoo which we call Lettuce. So I made her a little clay rabbit and painted it grey and white, just like Lettuce. The ears went a bit floppy but Lucy said she loved the rabbit even so.

I've done my best with everyone's presents. I've knitted another scarf for Gran, and hemmed a pocket handkerchief for Uncle Albert. I've painted a special watercolour picture of our Red Bookshop for Dad and threaded a red glass bead necklace for Rose. I've tried extra hard to make the perfect present for Ruby. I got friendly with our craft teacher and she's helped me make two twin rag-dolls – one with short hair and one with neat plaits. I've given them identical clothes, but I've made the one with short hair have a few little patches on her jeans and sewn a purple bruise or two on her arms. I've put Velcro inside their hands, so that even when they hug each other they really cling together.

She's here! It's so great! And yet it was really truly weird at Hineford because I saw this girl struggling off the train and just for a moment I didn't recognize Garnet! She looks exactly the same, I suppose, and she's still got her funny little plaits – but somehow she seems bigger and she's turned ever so posh too. I thought it was just her ridiculous school uniform, but even when we were home and she'd changed into a sweatshirt and jeans she still seemed different. And her voice! That truly is different. She sounds as if she's got a plum in her mouth and she uses all these la-di-da expressions.

'What are you talking like that for?' I asked.

'What do you mean?' she said, like she didn't know she was doing it.

'You haven't gone all snobby on me just because you go to that posh school?' I said.

'Don't be so daft,' she said, suddenly the old Garnet.

She put her arms around me tight and gave me a big hug.

'Oh Ruby, I've missed you so much!' she said.

I was suddenly so choked up I couldn't say a word in case I burst into babyish tears.

I'm home and it's quite wonderful! It's so fantastic to be back. It feels like I've been away for years and years. Dad and Rose were so pleased to see me – and Gran is coming to stay at the weekend, hurray. And of course, best of all, I'm back with Ruby. Oh, it feels so good to be with her. I realize that I've just felt like half of myself at Marnock Heights. She's exactly the same, with her hair sticking up all over the place. It looks kind of cool. She makes me feel terribly prim and proper and old-fashioned now.

I don't think she's missed me much. She hasn't said so anyway. She's just talked nineteen to the dozen about all these boys she knows. She goes everywhere with Blob now. Plus she's got heaps of friends at her drama class. I tried to tell her about Lucy and her rabbit, and Jamilla and all the other girls, but I think I must have been a bit boring because she started yawning and rolling her eyes. I shut up quickly. I don't want to upset her right at the start of the holidays.

It was great when we went to bed and we could talk in our twin language and replay all our secret games. Then it suddenly seemed as though the last few months had never happened.

I love having Garnet here – but she doesn't half get on my nerves sometimes. Dad and Rose are all over her, wanting to hear every teeny-tiny detail about her life at Marnock Heights. And Gran's even worse. She came to stay for Christmas today and she hardly took any notice of me whatsoever. She was all, 'Oh Garnet, your hair looks so pretty and tidy in your neat plaits' and 'You keep your clothes so nicely, dear, they all look new' and 'You speak really beautifully now, it's a treat just to listen to you.'

She doesn't say, 'Oh Ruby, your hair's such a mess' and 'You're such a terrible scruffbag' and 'You mumble and use slang and silly words' but it's obvious that's what she means. Garnet is definitely the favourite now. It's not that I'm jealous or anything. I mean, I'd much sooner be me. But I can't help feeling that my entire family are starting to take me for granted. Still, see if I care. I've got Blob and all his gang and we have the best fun ever. Blob doesn't like Garnet best.

Oh dear, Ruby wanted to go and hang out with that Blob today. I went along too, because I want to be with her all the time – but it was awful. Ruby and Blob and all those other boys hang about at the bus shelter and climb up on the roof and yell rude words at people. I tried to climb up too, just to show I'm willing, but I'm useless at it – and I didn't dare shout at anyone. I don't see the point. Then they all started jeering at me, even Ruby. I was scared I was going to burst into tears, but I stuck my nose in the air and pretended I didn't care.

'You're all pathetically infantile,' I said.

I hoped I'd squash them, but they all started saying worse things, and eventually I walked off back to the bookshop. I hoped Ruby would come running after me, but she didn't.

Dad and Rose and Gran asked where Ruby had got to when I went back.

'Oh, she's just hanging out with her friends,' I said. 'She'll be back later.'

Rose put her arm round me.

'Didn't they want you to hang out with them too?' she said.

'Oh, yes. They were very nice to me,' I said quickly.

'Those boys don't sound very nice at all,' said Gran. 'If I had my way I'd stop young Ruby running wild with them. But I know some people believe in letting young kiddies do exactly as they please.'

This was a dig at Rose. Gran still isn't very keen on her, though Rose tries very hard to be friendly. The way I'm trying very hard to be friendly with Ruby. But it's not working. When she came home last night, Gran said straight out, 'What are you doing, getting into trouble with all those awful boys, instead of playing sensibly with your sister?'

Ruby glared at me, thinking I'd been telling tales. And now I don't think she's speaking to me.

I can't believe Garnet can be so mean. She's changed so much. She never used to tell tales on me. She used to join in all the fun and do whatever I said. Now she just sticks her snobby nose in the air and acts like she's too good for us. Well, see if I care.

I don't know what to do. I thought Ruby and I would have such a brilliant time together these holidays, but it's not working. She barely talks to me. I just hope Christmas Day will make everything come right. I do hopes she likes her dolls – but maybe she'll think them babyish and pathetic.

I don't know what to do. Garnet's put all these beautifully wrapped presents under the Christmas tree. I was going to ask her if I could add my name, but now she's barely talking to me it's a bit awkward.

And there's a lumpy parcel especially for me. I haven't got her anything.

I was moping about in the kitchen, while Dad was in the shop and Gran and little goody-goody Garnet were sewing together in the living room. Rose caught me digging a little hole in the foundations of Gran's Christmas cake, scooping out fingerfuls of marzipan. I thought she'd get cross – but she came and dug out a little mouthful herself.

'I won't tell if you won't,' she said. 'Oh heavens, it's scrumptious, isn't it? Your Gran does everything so superbly. She's heaps better at everything. It makes me really irritated. Is that bad of me?'

'Imagine how irritated I feel, with genius goody-goody Garnet as my sister. Oh, Rose – she's got me a present and I haven't got her anything. Or anyone else for that matter. Garnet always organizes the present stuff, but she hasn't been here.'

'I'll help you with your Christmas presents, Ruby,' said Rose, going to the cupboard and getting out flour and sugar and ginger. 'Fancy making gingerbread biscuits? Little gingerbread people. You could do a pair of twins especially for Garnet.'

'Gingerbread biscuits aren't really proper presents though,' I said.

'It's the thought that counts. I think Garnet would be thrilled if you made her something special,' said Rose.

'I'm not so sure. I think she just looks down her nose at me now. She's changed now she goes to this posh school,' I said.

'Rubbish! She's just the same sweet girl she's ever been. You're the one who's all prickly and stand-offish. You've been acting like a royal pain ever since she came home.'

'So why are you being nice to me?'

'Because I care about you, dopey,' said Rose.

'What, more than Garnet?'

'I love you both the same. But you can be more fun sometimes, even though you give me more grief,' said Rose. 'Now come on, let's get cracking.'

So I made a whole family of gingerbread people. I tried specially hard to make two gingerbread girls. One had very neat twisty plaits and a smile. The other had mad hair and a scowl. I tried very hard with Rose's gingerbread lady, piping an icing sugar rose on her chest. Now they're all hidden away in a tin and I'll give them out on Christmas morning.

Oh, it's been such a wonderful Christmas! I woke up very early and Ruby woke up at exactly the same moment and we both whispered 'Happy Christmas' and then did our special twin grin. It was as if we were back to being us. We all opened our presents after breakfast. Gran's made us seriously embarrassing jumpers with little fluffy sheep on. My sheep are white and Ruby's black.

'Oh ha ha,' said Ruby. 'So I'm the black sheep of the family, Gran!'

'Not ha ha, it's baa baa,' I said. It wasn't very funny but Ruby laughed.

She handed out all these fantastic gingerbread biscuits as her Christmas presents. I got two, twin girls just like us.

'Eat them up then,' said Ruby.

'No!' I said.

'Why? Don't you like them?' Ruby paused. 'Do you
think they're infantile?'

'No! I like them so much I want to keep them for ever,'
I said. 'Now, you open my present for you, Ruby. I think
it really is a bit infantile. You'll probably laugh at me.'

Ruby tore the paper off the twin rag dolls and stared
at them.

'There! They're silly, aren't they? I mean, I know you
don't play with dolls anymore, obviously.'

'I'm not going to play with these either,' said Ruby,
gruffly.

'It's OK, I understand,' I said, thought I felt crushed.

'I'm going to put them on the windowsill in our
bedroom, and that way they won't ever get mucked up,
because I'm going to keep them for ever,' said Ruby.

We had a little hug, just like the little dolls, clinging as if we were made of Velcro too.

It was a seriously ace Christmas. Garnet liked my gingerbread twins and I love my little dolls. And Dad and Rose gave me a skate board, how wicked is that?! They gave Garnet a whole load of boring old books and some felt tips and a sketch pad, but she didn't seem to mind that I got the best present ever.

After Christmas dinner I wanted to go out straight away and try out my skate board. Garnet came with me and we went up to the top of the road and then practised whizzing down it. I had the most goes because it was my skate board – and Garnet was a bit rubbish at it actually.

Blob came riding up with Ferret-Face, both of them on new bikes. They thought my skate board was wicked too, so I let them have a go. Ferret-Face careered right into Garnet and nearly sent her flying. They all laughed.

'Whoops! Sorry, Your Royal Highness. How infantile of me!' said Ferret-Face.

'Don't you take the mick out of my sister!' I said,

 giving him a shove. 'Come on, Garnet, let's go home. I'll see you guys later.'

'It's OK, Ruby, really.'

'No, I'd sooner go back home. We'll draw with your new felt tips. I'll do some of my jokey cartoons.'

So we did just that, my twin and me. And it's OK OK OK, because we're back to being Ruby-and-Garnet again.

It was so sad saying goodbye to Ruby when I had to go back to Marnock Heights. I cried and cried and cried. Ruby cried too, though she screwed up her eyes and pretended she was fine.

'Never mind, you girls,' said Dad. 'It'll be Easter before you know it.'

I'm going to get started on my Easter presents already. I'm going to sew Easter bunnies for everyone. Twin bunnies for Ruby.

I do miss Garnet soooo much. But she'll be back for Easter and then we'll have such fun, Garnet and me. That's the great thing about being a twin. You can be separated for month after month, and then it feels a bit weird when you get back together again – but you know that underneath you're still best ever friends for ever, no matter what. Garnet and me. We might look different, but inside we're absolutely identical.

* RUBY AND GARNET'S * GINGERBREAD TWINS!

People have been baking gingerbread for more than a thousand years, and some people believe that Queen Elizabeth I served gingerbread men to important guests in the sixteenth century! Now gingerbread is especially popular at Christmas, and makes a tasty homemade present.

For your gingerbread twins:
- 350g plain flour, plus a bit extra for dusting
- 1 tsp bicarbonate of soda
- 2 tsp ground ginger
- 1 tsp ground cinnamon
- 125g butter
- 175g brown sugar
- 1 large egg
- 4 tbsp golden syrup

For the decorations:
- Icing in whatever colours you like!

What to do:
1. Preheat the oven to 180°C.

2. Line two baking trays with greaseproof paper.

3. Mix the flour, bicarbonate of soda, ginger, cinnamon and butter, and whizz in a food processor until you have a mixture that looks like breadcrumbs.

4. Stir in the sugar.

5. Beat the egg and golden syrup together and add to the food processor. Whizz again until the mixture clumps together.

6. Tip the dough out onto a clean surface. Knead until smooth, wrap in clingfilm and leave to chill in the fridge for 15 minutes.

7. Roll the dough out on a surface lightly dusted with flour, so that it's about half a centimetre thick. Using cutters, cut out the gingerbread twin shapes and place carefully on the baking tray, leaving a gap between them.

8. Bake for 12–15 minutes, or until lightly golden-brown. Leave on the tray for 10 minutes and then move to a wire rack to finish cooling.

9. When cooled, put your little figures into pairs, and decorate with the icing. You could make each set of twins identical – or, like Ruby and Garnet, you might want to make one a bit more untidy than her sister . . .

HETTY FEATHER'S
CHRISTMAS

I got very excited and enthusiastic about Christmas. It had never been an extraordinary occasion at the hospital. We'd each been given a penny and an orange – that was the extent of our Christmas gifts. There had been no lessons, no hours of darning, but there had been a punishingly long session in the chapel that gave us all aching backs and pins and needles in our dangling legs.

I had read about Christmas though, and was convinced that all other folk sat down to huge tables groaning with capons and figgy puddings galore, with a Christmas tree and coloured lanterns and many presents.

I looked around our small, dimly lit cottage, saw our big stewing pot, and sighed at the few coins rattling in my purse. 'How can we make Christmas special, Jem?' I wailed.

'We don't really set so much store by Christmas,' he said. 'Perhaps we can have a bit of stewing beef. That'll make a nice change.'

'It should be a roast,' I wailed. 'And I need to decorate the house to make it pretty. But what are we going to do about presents? I want to give real gifts. Folk will be getting tired of me stitching them silly clothes.'

'Oh, Hetty, you stitch beautiful clothes. We don't really give elaborate gifts – but I do have a tiny present for you.'

'Really? What is it?'

'You'll have to wait until Christmas Day! And listen – perhaps one of the girls will invite us to her house. Both Bess and Eliza have big ovens, so we could share their roast. We could bundle Mother up and drive her over in Molly's donkey cart,' said Jem, a little doubtfully, because both sisters lived miles away.

There were certainly a flurry of letters inviting us over for Christmas, and Mother seemed excited by the idea. But when Jem and I talked it over together, it didn't seem at all practical. It was getting so cold. Mother would freeze to death on the journey, even if we wrapped her up in twenty blankets. We couldn't take her special wheeled chair too, so she would be trapped in a corner – and would there be room enough for her in any spare bed?

It was dear Janet who solved our problem. 'You must come to our house for Christmas Day,' she said. 'I'm sure Jem and Father could give Peg a chairlift to our house. We have a big oven, and you know how much my mother loves cooking. Please say you'll come, Jem and Hetty.'

I think we were both torn. I wanted to have a wonderful Christmas in our house, and that was what Jem seemed to want too. If only our walls could expand so I could invite the Maples and many other guests besides. Perhaps not my foster sisters. I'd seen a little too much of them at the funeral.

I'd have liked to invite my father for Christmas. Katherine and Mina and Ezra could have smokies and baked cod and fishy pudding back where they belonged. I'd have liked my dear friend Freda the Female Giant to come too, though we might have to raise the ceiling specially. I'd have liked to see my pal Bertie the butcher's boy too, and he would surely bring us a fine turkey or a side of beef, but I wasn't so sure Jem would enjoy his company. And oh, most of all I'd have liked to send an invitation up to Heaven and have Mama pop down for the day. I'd make her a feast even better than manna, whatever that was. I just knew it was the only food they seemed to eat in Heaven. I paused, trying to decide what Mama would most like to eat during her visit.

'Hetty?' said Jem. He gave me a little nudge.

'I'm sorry,' he said to Janet. 'She's got that look in her eye. I think she's picturing again.'

'Don't tease me, you two,' I said, coming back to my senses. 'It's so kind of you and your family to invite us for Christmas, Janet. We'd love to come, wouldn't we, Jem?'

So that's what we did. It was all very jolly and we ate like kings. Mother particularly enjoyed herself. Mrs Maple was so kind to her. She'd made up a special chair like a throne, with extra cushions and blankets and shawls, and gave her a special Christmas meal tactfully cut into tiny pieces.

Mother was learning how to feed herself again now, though her hands were very shaky and she sometimes lost concentration halfway to her mouth. She couldn't help making a mess on the tablecloth and looked upset, but Mrs Maple patted her shoulder and said calmly, 'Don't fret, Peg dear, you're doing splendidly.'

We ate turkey, the very first time I'd tasted it. I didn't care for the live birds at all, with their weird worm-pink heads and fat feathery bodies and yellow claws. I always skirted round the turkey shed, keeping my distance. I'd had no idea that such a grotesque creature could taste so sweet and succulent. We had roast potatoes too, crisp and golden, and parsnips and carrots and small green sprouts like baby cabbages.

We ate until we were nearly bursting, but when we were offered a second serving we said yes please and Mother nodded enthusiastically. There were puddings too – a rich figgy pudding with a custard, a pink blancmange like a fairy castle, and a treacle tart with whipped cream. I could not choose which pudding I wanted because they all looked so wonderful, so I had a portion of each. This was a serious mistake, as I was wearing my first proper grown-up corset for the occasion. I'd bought it in the hope that squeezing my stomach in with its strong whalebone might help a little bust to pop out at the top, but I remained disappointingly flat-chested – and unable to breathe properly into the bargain.

I was glad I hadn't tried to encase Mother in her own corsets. She spread comfortably underneath her loose gown. She usually fell fast asleep after a big meal, but she stayed wide awake for the present giving. The Maples gave her a specially wrapped little package. I helped her unwrap it. Mr Maple had carved her special cutlery, cleverly designed to help her manage more efficiently. The spoon had a deep bowl to prevent spillage, the fork had clever prongs for easy spearing, and the knife had a curved handle so that Mother could grip it.

She seized hold of her spoon and fork, wanting to try them out immediately, so Mrs Maple gave her another bowl of figgy pudding, even though she was already full to the brim.

Of course, Mother had no presents to give the Maples in return, but Jem and I had done our best.

Jem gave me several shillings from his farm wages and I bought them an ornament at the market – a little china model of a house, not unlike their own, with a little lumpy extra bacon room beside the chimney. There was a message written carefully across the plinth: Bless This House.

I'd wanted to find something special for Janet too, because she had been such a dear friend, so I bought her a special pen. It was a fine one, with a green mottled casing, and I rather wanted it for myself, but I decided to be generous.

The Maples were very satisfyingly pleased with their presents. Janet hugged me hard and said she would use her beautiful pen every day and think of me.

'Then at least your journal will have variety,' I said. 'You can write *Today I got up – and I love my friend Hetty!*'

Jem and Mother and I had kept our presents to give to each other at the Maples'. I didn't want to fob Mother off with yet another nightgown. I bought her a new china washing jug and bowl, white with pink babies playing all around the inside. There was also a matching chamber pot, though it seemed a shame to piddle on the little children. I kept the pot at home because it might have been embarrassing unwrapping it in company.

I couldn't wait for Jem to open his present from me. Market Jim had let me have an end roll of scarlet worsted because it had a flaw running through the weave. I cut it out carefully on the slant and avoided the flaw altogether. I'd made it into a waistcoat with pockets and brass buttons.

'Oh, I say!' said Jem, going as red as the cloth when he unwrapped the waistcoat. 'I shall look a right robin redbreast! Oh, Hetty, it's the finest waistcoat I've ever seen. I shall wear it every Sunday.'

'You don't think it's too bright?' I asked anxiously.

'Not at all – the brighter the better,' said Jem, though I'm not entirely sure he was being truthful.

'Try your waistcoat on, Jem!' said Janet.

'Yes, do – I need to see if it fits properly,' I said.

'I probably won't be able to get the buttons done up because I've had so much Christmas dinner,' said Jem – but they slid easily into place. Although it sounds dreadfully like boasting, his waistcoat looked magnificent. Even taciturn Mr Maple murmured that it was a tremendous fit.

'But I wish I knew what the time was,' I said excitedly.

They all stared at me. The Maples' brass clock was ticking steadily on the mantelpiece.

'I'd like to check the time,' I said. 'Doesn't anyone else have a timepiece, Jem? Don't gentlemen keep a pocket watch about their person?'

'You know very well I don't have a pocket watch, Hetty,' said Jem.

'Not even in your fine new waistcoat?' I said. 'Why don't you check the pockets?'

Jem stared at me, and then slid his fingers into the slim pocket at the front. His hand felt something. His mouth fell open as he drew out a gold fob watch. It wasn't real gold, it was pinchbeck, and it wasn't brand new. I'd seen it on a curiosity stall in the market and I'd bargained hard for it. It was truly a pretty ordinary watch and it didn't even have a chain, but Jem cradled it in his hand as if it were part of the crown jewels.

'Oh, Hetty,' he whispered. 'Oh, Hetty!'

'Do you like it? I thought it was time you had a watch. Now you haven't any excuse to be late home and keep supper waiting,' I joked.

'I've never had such a splendid present,' said Jem. 'Thank you so much. Thank you so very, very much. Oh dear, I wish I'd got you something as special.' He handed me a tiny parcel apologetically.

I felt it carefully. 'Is it . . . jewellery?' I asked, my heart beating fast.

Janet gave a little gasp. 'Oh, Hetty, open it!'

I picked the paper open and saw a little necklace.

It was a silver sixpence with a hole bored into it so that it could hang on a dainty silver chain. 'Oh, Jem, it's lovely!' I whispered, putting it round my neck and fumbling with the clasp.

'Here, let me,' he said. 'It's an odd plain thing, I know – but you lost your last sixpence, the one I gave you as a token when you had to go off to the hospital. I thought you could keep this one hanging safe around your neck.' He fastened it in place for me. 'Perhaps it's just a silly whim. It's not very fancy like a real necklace,' he said uncertainly.

'It's perfectly lovely, Jem. I shall treasure it for ever,' I said.

✳ A VICTORIAN CHRISTMAS ✳

Lots of the Christmas traditions we have today come from the Victorian era, when Hetty Feather would have celebrated Christmas. Some of these traditions can be traced right back to Queen Victoria and her husband, Prince Albert, who had grown up in Germany. Some people think the huge success of a famous Victorian novel – *A Christmas Carol*, by Charles Dickens – meant that lots of the traditions mentioned in that story became very popular, and would be celebrated years and years on!

Before Queen Victoria, most people didn't have a Christmas tree in the UK. When she married Prince Albert, a newspaper published a drawing of the royal family celebrating around a decorated tree – a tradition that Prince Albert knew from his childhood in Germany. More and more families decided to copy the idea for themselves, and soon every home had its own tree covered in fruit and sweets, gifts and candles.

Up to then, presents had traditionally been given at New Year, but this changed as Christmas became more important to the Victorians – and as presents became bigger! To begin with, people gave small gifts like sweets, nuts and handmade toys and trinkets, and these were hung on the tree itself. As presents became bigger, people started to wrap them and place them underneath the tree instead.

The first Christmas cards were invented by a Victorian named Henry Cole in 1843. He asked his friend John Horsley, an artist, to draw the picture for the front of the card: a family enjoying Christmas dinner together, and people helping the poor. Henry and John then sold the cards for a few pence each, and within a few years, the tradition of sending a card to family and friends at Christmas had taken off.

The famous Christmas cracker is a Victorian invention, too! Tom Smith, a sweetmaker, noticed packages of sugared almonds wrapped in twists of paper when he visited Paris in 1848. They gave him the idea of the cracker: small packages full of sweets that would burst apart when pulled! Later, the sweets were replaced with paper hats, jokes and small gifts.

STARRING
TRACY BEAKER

I'm Tracy Beaker. Mark the name. I'll be famous one day.

I live in a children's home. We all call it the Dumping Ground. We're dumped here because no one wants us.

The Dumping Ground

No, that's total rubbish. My mum wants me. It's just she's this famous film star and she's way too busy making movies in Hollywood to look after me. But my mum's coming to see me at Christmas. She *is*. I just know she is.

'Your mum's not coming to see you in a month of Sundays,' said Justine Littlewood. 'Your mum's never ever coming back because she doesn't want anything to do with an ugly manky bad-mouthed stupid show-off who wets the bed every ni—'

She never managed to finish her sentence because I leaped across the room, seized hold of her hair and yanked hard, as if I was gardening and her hair was a particularly annoying weed.

Cam

I ended up in the Quiet Room. I didn't care. It gave me time to contemplate. That's a posh word for think. I have an extensive vocabulary. I am definitely destined to be a writer. A *successful* glossy rich and famous writer, not a struggling scruffy hack like Cam.

I mused (*another* posh word for think!) over the idea of a month of Sundays.

It would be seriously cool to have a lie-in every single day and watch telly all morning and have a special roast dinner and never have to go to school. But then I pondered (posh alternative number *three*) on the really bad thing about Sundays. Lots of the kids in the Dumping Ground get taken out by their mums or dads.

I don't. Well, I see Cam now, that's all. Cam's maybe going to be my foster mum. She's going to classes to see if she's suitable. It's mad. I don't trust my stupid social worker, Elaine the Pain. I don't want Cam to get cold feet. Though she keeps her toes cosy in her knitted stripy socks. She's not what you'd call a natty dresser. She's OK. But a foster mum isn't like a *real* mum. Especially not a famous glamorous movie star

Elaine the Pain

mum like mine. It isn't *her* fault she hasn't shown up recently. She's got such a punishing film schedule that, try as she might, she simply can't manage to jump on a plane and fly over here.

But she *is* going to come for Christmas, so there, Justine Now-Almost-Bald-And-It-Serves-You-Right Littlewood. My mum promised. She really really did.

She was going to see me in the summer. We were going to have this incredible holiday together on a tropical island, lying on golden sands in our bikinis, swimming with dolphins in an azure sea, sipping cocktails in our ten-star hotel . . .

Well, she was going to take me out for the day. It was all arranged. Elaine the Pain set it all up – but my poor mum couldn't make it. Right at the last minute she was needed for some live television interview – I'm sure that was it. Or maybe *Hello!* or *OK!* magazine wanted an exclusive photo shoot. Whatever.

So she never showed up, and instead of being understanding I heard Elaine ranting on to Jenny at the Dumping Ground, telling her all sorts of stupid stuff, like I was crying my eyes out. That was a downright lie. I would never cry. I sometimes get a little attack of hay fever, but I never cry.

I felt *mortified*. I wanted to cement Elaine's mouth shut. We had words. Quite a few of mine were bad words. I told Elaine that she had no business talking about one of her clients – i.e. me – and I had a good mind to report her. It was outrageous of her  slandering my mum. She was a famous Hollywood movie actress, didn't she *understand*? Elaine should be more *deferential*, seeing as she's just a poxy social worker.

Elaine said a bad word then. She said she understood why I was so angry. It was easier for me to take my anger out on her when I was *really* angry at my mum for letting me down yet again. *WHAT???* I wasn't the slightest bit angry with my mum. It wasn't her fault she's so popular and famous and in demand.

 'Yeah, so why haven't we ever seen her in a single film or telly show, and why are there never any photos of her in any of the magazines?' said Justine Why-Won't-She-Mind-Her-Own-Business Littlewood.

'Wash your ears out, Justine Littlewood. My mum's a famous *Hollywood* actress. Like, Hollywood in America. She isn't in films and mags over *here*, but in America she's incredibly well known. She can't set foot outside the door without the photographers snapping away and all her fans begging for autographs.'

'Yeah, yeah, she signs all these autographs, yet when does she ever bother to write to you?' said Justine Won't-Ever-Quit Littlewood.

But ha ha, sucks to you, J.L., because my mum *did* write, didn't she? She sent me a postcard.

She really did.

I keep it pinned on my wall, beside the photo of Mum and me when I was a baby and still looked sweet. The postcard had a picture of this cutesie-pie teddy with two teardrops falling out of his glass eyes and wetting his fur and the word *Sorry!* in sparkly lettering.

On the back my mum wrote:

So sorry I couldn't make it, Tracy.
Chin up, chickie! See you soon.
Christmas?
          Lots of love,
                    Mum
                    xxx

I know it off by heart. I've made up a little tune and I sing it to myself every morning when I wake up and every night when I go to bed. I sing it softly in school. I sing it when I'm watching television. I sing it in the bath. I sing it on the toilet. I sing the punctuation and stuff too, like: *'Christ-mas, question mark. Lots of love, comma, Mum, kiss kiss kiss.'* It's a very catchy tune. I might well be a song writer when I grow up as well as a famous novelist.

Of course I'm also going to be an actress just like my mum. I am soon going to be acclaimed as a brilliant child star. I have the ☆STAR☆ part in a major production this Christmas. Truly.

I am in our school's play of *A Christmas Carol*.

I haven't done too well in casting sessions in the past. At my other schools I never seemed to get picked for any really juicy roles. I was a donkey when we did a Nativity play. I was a little miffed that I wasn't Mary or the Angel Gabriel at the very least, but like a true little trooper I decided to make the most of my part.

I worked hard on developing authentic eeyore donkey noises. I eeyored like an entire herd of donkeys during the performance. OK, I maybe drowned out Mary's speech, and the Angel Gabriel's too (to say nothing of Joseph, the Innkeeper, the Three Wise Men and Assorted Shepherds), but real donkeys don't wait politely till people have finished talking, they eeyore whenever they feel like it. I felt like eeyoring constantly, so I did.

I didn't get picked to be in any more plays at that stupid old school. But this school's not too bad. We have a special art and drama teacher, Miss Simpkins. She understands  that if we do art we need to be dead artistic and if we do drama then we should aim at being dead *dramatic*. She admired my arty paintings of Justine Littlewood being devoured by lions and tigers and bears.

'You're a very imaginative and lively girl, Tracy,' said Miss Simpkins.

I wasn't totally bowled over by this. That's the way social workers talk when they're trying to boost your confidence or sell you to prospective foster carers. 'Imaginative and lively' means you get up to all sorts of irritating and annoying tricks. *Me?* Well, maybe.

My famous imagination ran away with me when we were auditioning for *A Christmas Carol*. I didn't really know the story that well. It's ever so l-o-n-g and I'm a very busy person, with no time to read dull old books. Miss Simpkins gave us a quick précis version and I had a little fidget and yawn because it seemed so old fashioned and boring, but my ears pricked up – right out of my curls – when she said there were ghosts.

'I'll be a ghost, Miss. I'm great at scaring people. Look, look, I'm a headless ghost!' I pulled my school jumper up over my head and held my arms like claws and went, 'Whooooo!'

Silly little Peter Ingham squealed in terror and ducked under his desk.

'See, I can be really convincing, Miss! And I can do you all sorts of *different* ghosts. I can do your standard white-sheet spooky job, or I can moan and clank chains, or I could paint myself grey all over and be this wafting spirit ghost creeping up on people, ready to leap out at them.'

I leaped out at Weedy Peter just as he emerged from under his desk. He shrieked and ducked, banging his head in the process.

'Well, you're certainly entering into the spirit

of things, Tracy,' said Miss Simpkins, bending down to rub Peter's head and give the little weed a cuddle. 'There now, Peter, don't look so scared. It isn't a real ghost, it's only Tracy Beaker.'

'I'm scared of Tracy Beaker,' said Peter. 'Even though she's my friend.'

I wish the little creep wouldn't go around telling everyone he's my friend. It's dead embarrassing. I don't want you to think he's my *only* friend. I've got heaps and heaps of friends. Well. Louise isn't my best friend any more. She's gone totally off her head because she now wants to be friends with Justine No-Fun-At-All Littlewood. There's no one in our class who actually quite measures up to my friendship requirements.

Hey, I *have* got a best friend. It's Cam! She comes to see me every Saturday. She's not like my mum, glamorous and beautiful and exciting. But she can sometimes be good fun. So she's my best friend. And Miss Simpkins can be my second best friend at school.

Peter's just my friend at the Dumping Ground. Especially at night time, when there's no one else around.

Peter seemed to be thinking about our night-time get-togethers too.

'Promise promise promise you won't pretend to be a ghost tonight, Tracy?' he whispered anxiously.

'Ah! I'm afraid I can't possibly promise, Peter. I am the child of a famous Hollywood star. I take my acting seriously. I might well have to stay in character and act ghostly all the time,' I said.

'Maybe we'd better cast you as something else, Tracy,' said Miss Simpkins.

'Oh no, *please* let me be the ghost!' I begged.

It turned out there were four main ghosts in *A Christmas Carol* and a motley crew of ghostly extras too.

There was the Ghost of Christmas Past.

'Let *me* be the Ghost of Christmas Past, Miss Simpkins,' I said.

Louise

'No, Tracy, I need a girl with long fair hair to be the Ghost of Christmas Past,' said Miss Simpkins.

She chose *Louise*.

'Now there's the Ghost of

Christmas Present,' said Miss Simpkins.

'Let *me* be the Ghost of Christmas Present,' I said.

'No, Tracy. I need a big jolly boy to be the Ghost of Christmas Present,' said Miss Simpkins.

Freddy

She chose old Fatty Freddy.

'Now there's the Ghost of Christmas Yet to Come,' said Miss Simpkins.

'I thought Charles Dickens was meant to be a good writer. He's a bit repetitive when it comes to ghosts, isn't he?' I said. 'Still, let *me* be the Ghost of Christmas Yet to Come.'

Philip

'No, Tracy, I need a very tall boy to be the Ghost of Christmas Yet to Come,' said Miss Simpkins.

She chose this pea-brained boy called Philip who couldn't haunt so much as a graveyard.

'There's just one more main ghost and that's Marley's Ghost,' said Miss Simpkins. 'He wails and clanks his chains.'

'Oooh, I'm a totally terrific wailer and clanker, you know I am! Let *me* be Marley's Ghost,' I begged.

'I'm very tempted, Tracy, but perhaps you might indulge in a tad too much wailing and clanking,' said Miss Simpkins.

Justine!

She chose *Justine Can't-Act-For-Toffee Littlewood*, who can't clank to save her life and can barely whimper, let alone give a good ghostly *wail*.

I was Severely Irritated with Miss Simpkins. I decided she wasn't my friend any more. I didn't want to be in her stupid play if she wouldn't pick me for one of the main ghosts. I didn't want to be one of the no-name *extra* ghosts or any of the other people – these silly Fezziwigs and Cratchits.

I turned my back on Miss Simpkins and whistled a festive tune to myself . . . with new lyrics.

'Jingle Bells, Miss Simpkins smells,
Jingle all the day.
Oh what a fart it is to take part
In her stupid Christmas play.'

'And now there's only one part left,' said Miss Simpkins. 'Are you listening to me, Tracy?'

I gave the tiniest shrug, slumping down in my seat. I tried to make it crystal clear that I wasn't remotely interested.

'I'll take that as a yes,' said Miss Simpkins cheerfully. 'Yes, there's just the part of crusty old Ebenezer Scrooge himself to cast. Now, I'm going to have serious problems. This is the key part of the whole play. The *best* part, the *leading* part. I need a consummate actor, one who isn't phased by a really big juicy part, one who can act bad temper and meanness and lack of generosity, and yet one who can convincingly thaw and repent and behave wonderfully after all. I wonder . . .'

I sat up straight. I gazed at Miss Simpkins. She surely couldn't mean . . .

'You, Tracy Beaker! You will be my Scrooge!' she said.

'Yay!' I shrieked. I bounced up and down in my seat as if I had an india-rubber bottom.

'That's stupid, Miss!' said Justine Can't-Hold-Her-Tongue Littlewood. 'You can't let Tracy be Scrooge. Why should she get the best part? She just mucks around and doesn't take things seriously. You can't let her be in the play, she'll just mess it up for all of us.'

'I'll certainly mess *you* up,' I mumbled.

I rushed out of my seat, right up to Miss Simpkins.

'I'll take it all dead seriously, Miss Simpkins, I promise. You can count on me. And don't be surprised if I turn out to be unexpectedly brilliant at acting as my mum is a Hollywood movie star making one film after another.'

'As if!' said Louise.

'I know the only sort of movies Tracy Beaker's mum would star in. *Blue* movies!' said Justine Liar-Liar-Liar Littlewood.

My fists clenched, I so badly wanted to punch her straight in the nose, but I knew she was just trying to wind me up so Miss Simpkins would lose her temper with me and not let me be Scrooge after all. I simply raised my eyebrows and hissed a small rebuff along the lines that her dad belonged in a *horror* movie. Then I turned my back on her and smiled at Miss Simpkins.

'As I've got the biggest part you'd better give me a copy of the play straight away, Miss Simpkins, so I can get to be word perfect. In fact, maybe I ought to be excused all the boring lessons like literacy and maths just so I can concentrate on learning my part.'

'Nice try, Tracy, but I'm not that much of a pushover,' said Miss Simpkins. 'No, you'll have to learn your part in your own time.'

I was so anxious to play Scrooge I learned my lines in *other* people's time. Mostly Cam's. I used up two entire Saturday visits getting her to read out all the other parts while I Bah-Humbugged my way through Scrooge. Cam tried almost too hard at first, doing weird voices for all the Christmas ghosts and an extremely irritating little-boy lisp for Tiny Tim.

'Hey, *I'm* the one that's supposed to be acting, not you,' I said. 'Just *speak* the lines.'

'Look, I'm the adult. Aren't I the one supposed to tell *you* what to do?' said Cam, swatting me with the script of the play. 'Oh no, sorry, I forgot. You're Tracy Beaker so you get to be Big Bossy-Knickers, right?'

'Absolutely right, Cam. You got it in one! Hey, all this saying lines about sucking pigs and sausages has made me simply starving. Any chance of us going out to McDonald's?'

Mike

Jenny

I didn't just pester Cam to hear my lines. I got Jenny and Mike at the Dumping Ground to help me out, though I got dead annoyed when they wanted Justine Utter-Rubbish Littlewood and Louise and weedy little Peter to attend our special rehearsals too.

'It's not fair! I can't concentrate with all that rabble around,' I declared. 'Let's send them packing.'

'They're all in *A Christmas Carol* too, Tracy. You're not the only one who needs help with your lines,' said Jenny.

'We can act it all out together,' said Mike. 'Trust you to behave like a prima donna, Tracy.'

'Yeah, trust me, because what is the definition of prima donna, Mike? Isn't she the star of the whole show? I rest my case!'

I even considered commandeering Elaine the Pain to help me with my part. She's always encouraging us looked-after kids to role-play and act out our angst so I wondered if she might have any useful tips.

I'd lost it a little there. As if Old Elaine could

ever be useful at anything! Especially Elaine in Christmas mode, decking our ropy Dumping Ground with tinsel and home-made paper chains, a pair of wacky rainbow antlers bobbing manically on her head and a Comic Relief nose pinching her own. She was wearing a holly-berry-red knitted jumper and an ivy-green skirt, way too tight, and was warbling the words of 'Rudolph the Red-nosed Reindeer'.

'Elaine my social worker
Had a very large fat bum,
And if you ever saw her
You would scream out loud and run,'
I sang under my breath.

Not quite under enough. Elaine heard and got quite aerated. She burbled on about Cheek and Attitude and Silly Offensive Personal Remarks that could be Really Hurtful. I started to feel a little bit mean. I was even considering saying sorry. Elaine can't *help* having a huge bum after all.

She said she understood I was feeling tense and anxious because she'd heard I'd taken on a huge part in our school play when I simply wasn't used to Applying Myself and Being Responsible.

I stopped feeling even the tiniest bit sorry. I was glad when I heard Elaine say to Jenny, 'Look, can I ask you for a really honest answer? Do you think my bu— behind looks a bit big in my new skirt?'

I decided I would simply rely on myself and learn my part properly and show them all. This was fine and dandy during the day but not quite so easy at night. I kept having these bizarre nightmares where I was all alone on stage and I kept opening my mouth like a goldfish but no sound at all came out. I couldn't so much as blow a bubble. The audience started getting restless, pelting me with rotten fruit. One maggoty old apple landed straight in my gaping mouth, so I looked exactly like the Ghost of Christmas Present's sucking pig.

Then they put me on a spit and
screamed that I was burning so they t.
at me. Lots and lots of water . . . Wher
up my bed was unaccountably wet and I h.
go on a dismal damp trek to the bathroom and
the linen cupboard.

I met up with Weedy Peter
on a similar mission. He
was actually crying. Like I
said, I never cry. I might
occasionally have an attack
of hay fever but that is a
medical condition, not
an emotional state.

'What are you
blubbing for, silly?' I
asked.

'I'm so scared I'll be
rubbish in the school
Christmas play,' Peter
sobbed. 'I wish wish wish
Miss Simpkins hadn't made me be Tiny Tim. I
don't *want* to act. I can't remember the words
and I can't figure out which leg to hop on, and
it will all be so so so much worse with people
watching us. It's all right for you, Tracy. You

never get scared of anything and you're a terrible show-off so acting's right up your street.'

'Cheek! Don't you dare call me a terrible show-off!' I said.

'But you are.'

'Yes, I know, but you don't have to point it out.'

'I'd give *anything* to be a terrible show-off,' Peter said earnestly. 'Can't you show me how, Tracy? Is there a special trick?'

'It's just a natural gift, Peter,' I said. 'I was born showing off. I shot out of my mum and said, "Hi, folks!" to the doctor and the nurse, and then I turned a somersault, stood on my tiny feet and did a little tap dance on the delivery table.'

I felt for Peter's head in the dark. His mouth was hanging open. I closed it gently.

'Joke,' I said. 'OK, as an extra special favour to you, Peter, we'll act out all our scenes together.'

We started meeting up for midnight rehearsals on a regular basis. Peter was soon word perfect because he had hardly any lines to learn. I mean, how hard is it to remember 'God bless us, every one' for goodness sake? But though he could say the words he couldn't *act* them at all. He just mumbled them in a monotone.

'You certainly *are* rubbish at acting, Peter,' I said. 'Oh stop it, don't go all sniffly on me. I'm not being mean, I'm simply stating a fact. But don't worry, I'll help. You've got to feel your way into the part. You're this little weedy boy with a delicate constitution and a gammy leg. That's not hard, is it? Talk about type-casting.'

'I haven't got a gammy leg,' said Peter the Pedant.

'I'll kick it hard if you like,' I said. 'Now, even though you're down on your luck, you're a chirpy little soul, the favourite of your family. Your dad especially dotes on you.'

'I wish that bit was true,' said Peter mournfully.

'Yeah. Me too,' I said.

We huddled closer under our shared blanket.

'I wish I had a family to come and see me in the play,' said Peter. 'Well, maybe I don't – not if I'm rubbish.'

'You won't be rubbish, you'll be terrific with the

Totally Tremendous Tracy Beaker directing you. Yes, it's sad you haven't got anyone. Never mind, I'll ask my mum to give you a special wave.'

'Your mum's coming?' Peter asked, sounding astonished.

'You bet. She's coming for Christmas, she promised,' I said. 'She'll be desperate to watch me act to see if I've inherited her show-biz talents – which I *have*. I've written her a letter telling her all about the show.'

I'd written her several letters. In fact I wrote to her every single day and gave them to Jenny to post.

Dear Mum,

I can't wait to see you at Christmas, remember, you promised? Can you come a week early so you can come to my school play and see me in my {STAR} role as Scrooge? I am dead good at being a mean miserable old man.

Lots and lots and lots of love from your happy cheery little daughter

Tracy xxx

'I know just how much you want to see your mum, Tracy, but don't get *too* fixated on her coming to see you,' said Elaine.

'But she is, she wrote and said – she promised . . . practically.'

'I know how much you want her to come, but sometimes our wishes don't always come true,' said Elaine.

I wished I didn't have a social worker. I wished I had a fairy godmother who said, 'You want your mum to come and see you? Certainly, Tracy, no problem,' and she'd wave her wand and *wow! pow!* there would be my mum, all pink and powdery and perfect, her arms outstretched ready to give me a big hug.

I haven't got a fairy godmother. I have to work my own magic.

The next Saturday Cam came to see me at the Dumping Ground as usual. We had a quick run-through of the whole play – and I mean *quick*. I gabbled my way through my part like I was on fast forward. I possibly missed out whole chunks, but when Cam pointed this out I just said, 'Yeah, yeah, whatever, but I'm on *this* bit now,' and revved up into Thousand-Words-A-Minute Top Gear.

We finished the play in twenty minutes dead.

'Right! Done the rehearsal. Now let's go out,' I said.

'Ah! So McDonald's is calling?' said Cam.

'No. Well, *yes*, I'm starving actually, but I want to go round the shops. I want to do some Christmas shopping.'

Jenny gives all of us older kids a special Christmas shopping allowance. She goes shopping with the little kids and helps them choose – otherwise they just spend it on sweets for themselves. Us older kids usually snaffle a little for sweets too, but this time I wanted *all* my money for presents. One set of presents in particular.

'I might as well do my Christmas shopping too, Tracy,' said Cam.

'Ooh! What are you getting for me, Cam?' I asked, momentarily diverted. 'I could really do with some new jeans. Designer, natch. And one of those really cool furry jackets with a hood. And there's this seriously wicked motorized go-cart that would be fun for swooping all round the gardens of the Dumping Ground – *swoosh, swoosh* – Oh I'm *sorry*, Justine Littlewood, was that your foot?'

'Tracy, I can't afford to buy you so much as a motorized matchbox at the moment. I'm totally skint. You've got to adopt a new attitude. *It's the thought that counts.*'

'It strikes me *you* should be playing Scrooge, not me, if you're not giving proper Christmas presents,' I said. 'Honestly, Cam, why don't you get your act together and write a socking great bestseller? Something that would be snapped up by Hollywood in a million-dollar movie deal. Then me and my mum could star in it.'

'Dream on, sweetheart,' said Cam. 'I somehow don't think I'm bestseller material.'

'You've got to think positive, Cam. You've got to *make* your dreams come true,' I said.

I was intent on doing just that.

When we got to the shopping centre I got Cam to come to Boots with me to buy some really special make-up.

'So what's the *best* brand, Cam?' I asked.

'Don't ask me, Tracy, I hardly ever wear make-up. I just buy whatever's cheapest,' she said.

'Well, this is a present for my mum so I want the most glamorous gorgeous stuff possible.'

I fiddled around trying out different lipstick shades on my wrist until it looked like I had red-rose tattoos up both arms.

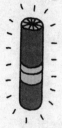

Then I finally selected the most perfect pearly pink.

Cam thought we were done.

'No, no! Hand lotion next!'

Cam sighed and fidgeted while I tried out all the lotions, sniffing them carefully and comparing them for creaminess. After a while my hands got very slippery and sticky and I had to wipe them on my skirt.

'I don't think Jenny's going to be very thrilled about those great greasy marks,' said Cam. 'Come *on*, Tracy, let's go to the bookshop now.'

'No, no, I've got to get my mum another present. I need a jewellery shop now.'

'But you've already got your mum the lipstick *and* the hand lotion.' Cam sneaked a peek in my purse. 'Don't forget you've got to buy Christmas presents for everyone.'

I wasn't interested in buying presents for everyone. I didn't want to buy a present for anyone but my *mum*.

I dragged Cam into a lovely sparkly jewellery shop, but when I saw the prices of even the weeniest rings I had to back away, sighing.

'That's real jewellery, Tracy. A little bit ostentatious, all that gold and diamonds. I think costume jewellery is much more tasteful,' Cam said quickly.

'OK. Where do you buy this costume jewellery then?'

She took me to the ground floor of this big department store and I walked round and round great glass cabinets of jewellery. I saw a pink heart on a crimson ribbon. It was utterly beautiful. I could just imagine it round my mum's neck. It was *very* expensive, even for costume jewellery, but I counted out every last penny in my purse and found I could just about manage it, keeping a fiver back for my last-of-all purchase.

'Are you *sure*, Tracy? I think maybe your mum would be happy with just the lipstick. Or the hand lotion.'

'My mum likes *lots* of presents,' I said. 'I know what I'm doing, Cam.'

I *didn't* really know what I was going to do about everyone else's presents. Still, I wasn't speaking to Louise any more on account of the fact she'd ganged up with Justine Ugly-Unscrupulous-Friend-Snatcher Littlewood so I didn't have to buy her anything.

There was Jenny and Mike, but they quite liked all that pathetic home-made calendar and dried-pasta-picture rubbish. Maybe Miss Simpkins at school would go for that sort of stuff too. Ditto Cam. She believed that it was the thought that counted, didn't she? She'd as good as indicated that I wasn't getting anything to speak of from her. It would only embarrass her if I gave her too lavish a gift.

That just left Weedy Peter. I was sure I could fob him off with something of mine I didn't want any more, like my leather wallet with the broken clasp or my leaky snowglobe or my wrinkly copy of *The Lion, the Witch and the Wardrobe* that got a little damp when I was reading it in the bath.

I heaved a sigh of relief. Christmas-present problem *sorted*. Now there was just one present left.

'Come on, Cam, I've got to go to a bookshop,' I said, tugging her.

She was peering at some very boring pearls in the jewellery cabinet.

'Bookshop! Now we're talking. But hang on. Look, what do you think of that little pearl necklace there – the one with the diamanté clasp? All the sparkly stuff's half price, special offer.'

'Cam, you are so *not* a pearl necklace person.'

'They're not for me, silly.'

I blinked at her. 'Look, Cam, it's very kind of you, but actually *I'm* not a pearl necklace person either.'

Cam snorted. 'You can say that again, Tracy. No no no, I'm thinking about my mum.'

'Ah. Yes. She's quite posh, isn't she, your mum?'

'Insufferably so. Very very much a pearl sort of person. But *real* pearls. These are fake so I expect she'd turn her nose up at them.'

'Well, get her real ones then.'

'Don't be a banana, Tracy. I couldn't possibly afford them. I can't actually afford the fake ones, even half price. You know, I'm like a fake daughter to my mum. She's *so* disappointed that I'm not all smart and glossy with a posh partner and a brilliant career.'

'Well, you could still try to get them,' I said doubtfully.

'I don't want to. I want to be *me*. It's so hard not to get wound up by my mum. I'm absolutely dreading going home for Christmas.'

'You're *dreading* going home for Christmas?' I said slowly.

Cam stopped gazing at the fake pearls and looked at me.

'Oh Tracy, I'm sorry. That was such a stupid tactless thing to say to you. I know just how much you want to see your mum this Christmas.'

'And I'm going to,' I said, very firmly and fiercely.

'Well, that would be truly great, but remember, your mum might just be busy or tied up or . . . or . . . abroad,' Cam said.

'No, she's going to be here. She's going to come and see me in my starring role in *A Christmas Carol*. And then she'll stay over. I dare say she'll take us to this top hotel and we'll have Christmas there. Yeah, it will be so great. We'll sleep in this big big queen-size bed and then we'll splash in our power shower and then we'll have the most immense breakfast. I'll be allowed to eat whatever I want. I can put six spoonfuls of sugar on my cereal and eat twenty sausages in one go and I'll have those puffy things with maple syrup—'

'Waffles?'

'Yeah, I'll scoffle a waffle,' I said as we walked out of the department store towards the bookshop. 'I'll scoffle *six* waffles and I'll have hot chocolate with whipped cream, and *then* I'll open my presents and my mum will give me heaps and heaps and heaps of stuff – a whole wardrobe of designer clothes, enough new shoes and trainers and boots to shod a giant centipede—'

'And a motorized go-cart? Sorry, a whole *fleet* of them.'

'Yep, and bikes and scooters and my own trampoline, and I'll be able to bounce soooo high I'll swoop straight up to the sky and everyone will look up at me and go, *Is it a bird? Is it a plane? Is it Superman? Is it Santa? Noooo, it's the Truly Tremendous Tracy Beaker!*'

I bounced up and down to demonstrate. I accidentally landed on Cam's foot and she gave a little scream, but she was very nice about it.

We carried on playing the Christmas game until we got to the bookshop. Well, it wasn't exactly a game. I knew it was all going to come true, though perhaps I was embellishing things a little. I am occasionally prone to exaggeration. That means I can get carried away and tell socking great lies. They start to seem so real that I believe them too.

Cam was very happy to be in the bookshop. She ran her finger lovingly along the long lines of paperbacks.

'I'll have a little browse,' she said. 'The children's section is over in that corner, Tracy.'

'I don't want the children's books. I want the classics section,' I said loftily.

'Oh yes?' said Cam. 'You fancy a quick flick through *War and Peace*?'

'That's quite a good title. If I write my true life story about my Dumping Ground experiences I'll call my book *War and More War and Yet More War*. No, I'm going to peruse the collected works of Mr Charles Dickens.'

That showed her. I wasn't kidding either. I wanted to find a copy of *A Christmas Carol*. I found a very nice paperback for £4.99. I had just one penny left. I didn't put it back in my purse. I decided to throw it in the dinky wishing well by the shopping centre Christmas tree.

I could do with a good wishing session.

Cam was still browsing in the fiction, her nose in a book, her whole expression one of yearning. I knew she couldn't afford all the books she wanted. She said she often spent ten or twenty minutes in the shop reading a book before putting it back reluctantly. Once she'd even marked her place with a bus ticket so she could sidle back the next day – and the next and the next and the next – until she'd finished the whole story.

I suddenly wished I'd saved just a little bit of my Christmas money to buy Cam a paperback. I fidgeted uncomfortably with my wishing penny. I threw it up and caught it again and again, practising my wishing. Then I dropped it and it rolled off, right round the shelves. I ran after it and practically bumped my nose on the MIND BODY SPIRIT sign.

I picked up my penny, my eyes glazing over at all these dippy books about star signs and spiritual auras – and then I saw a title in sparkly silver lettering: *Make Your Wishes Come True*.

I reached for the book, my hand shaking. It was a slim little book, written by someone called Grizelda Moonbeam, White Witch. I considered calling myself Tracy Moonbeam, Very Black Witch. I'd learn magic spells and make frogs and toads spew out of Justine Get-Everyone-On-Her-Side Littlewood.

I opened the book and started flipping through the pages. It really was full of spells! I couldn't find a frog-and-toad curse for your worst enemy, but there were plenty of love potions and magic charms. I turned another page and then my heart started thumping.

'CHARM TO BE WITH YOUR LOVED ONE ON A FESTIVE OCCASION'.

My mum was my Very Much Loved One and you couldn't get a more Festive Occasion than Christmas. I so badly wanted her to come this Christmas and watch me act Scrooge on stage I was about ready to pop.

I read the charm carefully. Grizelda advised mixing one part mead to two parts dandelion wine, adding cinnamon for spice and ginger for warmth and sugar for sweetness.  She suggested stirring the mixture well while chanting the Loved One's name, then drinking from the wrong side of the glass without drawing breath.

I blinked. Easy-peasy! I gabbled the ingredients over and over again. I'd got so used to learning my Scrooge lines that the recipe tucked itself neatly inside my head without too much fussing. Then I reverently replaced Grizelda Moonbeam, danced seven times around the bookshelf because it seemed a magic thing to do, and then staggered giddily off to find Cam.

'Are you feeling OK, Tracy?' she asked, as I bumped right into her.

'I'm fine,' I said, carefully sorting out my carrier bags *and* my penny. 'Come on, Cam, let's get cracking. I've got all my Christmas presents now.'

'And I haven't got a sausage,' said Cam, sighing. 'Oh well, maybe I can make some of my presents this year.'

I shook my head at her. 'Look, Cam, making presents is for little kids. *I* can barely get away with it. You're way too old, believe me. And forget *all* about it on my behalf. I want a proper present!'

'You don't really work hard to get people to like you, Tracy,' said Cam, shutting her book with a snap.

'I don't have to. I'm bubbling over with natural charm,' I said.

However, I pondered her point as we left the bookshop. What *was* all this gubbins about getting people to like you? I didn't fancy sucking up to people all the time and saying they looked lovely when they looked rubbish and all that sick-making nonsense. Louise was a past master at that – and a present mistress too. She could flutter her long eyelashes, fix you with a soulful glance with her big blue eyes and say softly that you were the funniest girl in all the world and she wanted to be your best friend for ever and you actually *believed* it, until she ganged up with Someone Else.

Still, I wouldn't want to be Louise's best friend any more. I don't *want* her to like me again. I definitely don't want Justine Dog-Breath-Snake-Tongue-Baboon-Bottom Littlewood to like me.

I don't need to work at getting people to like me. Heaps and heaps of people do. I go out of my way to *stop* Weedy Peter liking me. Elaine and Jenny and Mike like me too. They do heaps of things for me, don't they? Although they're paid to hang out with me. Maybe they simply can't stick me but don't tell me because it would be unprofessional.

It was silly thinking like this. I was starting to panic. It wasn't good for me to get so worked up, though of course all great actors were hypersensitive and temperamental. Miss Simpkins liked me or she wouldn't have offered me the starring part in her play. Unless . . . she was simply sorry for me because I was little Tracy No-Friends, the most unpopular girl in the whole school.

Maybe Cam didn't like me either. She just came to take me out every week as a duty. She was making a fuss of the Sad Ugly Kid with Mega Attitude Problems because it made her feel good. Maybe I was her Unpleasant Weekly Project, on a par with taking out the rubbish and cleaning the toilet.

'Tracy? Why are you breathing all funny?' said Cam, as we walked through the shopping centre.

'I'm hyperventilating on account of your hostile remarks,' I said, going extra gaspy to give her a fright.

'What do you mean?'

'You said no one likes me,' I said.

I suddenly couldn't *help* gasping I felt so horrible.

'I *didn't*!' Cam said.

'You did, you did, you did, and it's outrageous to say that to a looked-after child. You've probably traumatized me for life,' I said, giving her a shove.

I used my elbows and they're particularly sharp.

'Ouch! You've probably *punctured* me for life with your stiletto elbows.'

'Well, I'm fading away with hunger. It's no wonder I'm so skinny. You'd better whip me to McDonald's quick, what with my general anorexic state and my tragic realization that everyone totally hates me.'

'Oh Tracy, will you just *stop* it. I didn't say anyone hated you. I didn't say anyone didn't like you. I simply said you didn't try hard to make people like you.' Cam paused. She took hold of me by the shoulders, staring straight into my eyes. 'But even when you treat me like dirt *I* still like you.'

I relaxed.

'Mind you, I'd like you even more if you'd try being gentle and considerate and polite,' said Cam.

'*Me?*' I said. 'Dream on! Come on, I want my Big Mac and fries. Please. Dear kind pretty ever-so-nice-to-me Camilla.'

'Yuck! It was working till you said my name.

That's what my mum calls me. Oh God, I wish it wasn't nearly Christmas.'

I had my own wish to make. A real magic spell, *much* more powerful than throwing a penny in a polystyrene wishing well. I went over it in my head as I munched my burger and gobbled my chips and slurped my shake.

'Can we go back to your house for tea, Cam?' I asked. 'Hey, I've thought what I want for tea too.'

'You're only just having your lunch, girl.'

'Yeah, yeah, but I want something *special* for tea. Something Christmassy.'

'You know I'm pretty skint at the moment. I expect I can manage a sausage on a stick and a mince pie but that's about my limit.'

'Never mind that stuff. Well, yes to sausages and yes to mince pies too, and a chocolate log would be a good idea, come to think of it, but what I was really hoping for was Christmas punch.'

'What?'

'You know. A special festive drink. There's this amazing punch I've heard about. You mix one part mead to two parts dandelion wine, and then you add cinnamon and ginger and sugar, stir it all around, and Bob's your uncle, Fanny's your aunt, yummy yummy in your tummy.' I mimed being a cocktail barman for her and ended up with a flourish.

'Cheers!' I said, raising my imaginary glass.

Cam blinked at me. 'Well, personally I prefer a simple glass of wine as a festive drink, but each to their own. We can try and fix you something similar—'

'No, no, you can't muck about with the ingredients, it'll lose all its potency,' I said urgently.

Cam's eyes narrowed. 'Tracy, have you taken up witchcraft?'

She is so spooky at times. It's as if she can open a little flap in my head and peer straight into my mind.

'Watch out if I *am* a trainee witch, Cam. Think of the havoc I could wreak,' I said, contorting my face into a witchy grimace and making manic old-hag cackles.

'Help help help,' said Cam, raising her

eyebrows. 'OK, I'll see what we can do. Come on, let's have a trek round Sainsbury's and see what we can come up with.'

We couldn't find any mead at all *or* dandelion wine. I started to fuss considerably.

'It's OK, Tracy. Mead is a honey drink,' Cam told me. 'I've got a jar of honey at home so we'll put a spoonful of honey in a glass of wine, and pick a dandelion on the way home and chop it up and add it too, OK? I've got sugar and we'll buy a little pot of cinnamon and – what was the other thing? Oh, ginger. Well, I think I've got a packet of ginger biscuits somewhere. They might be a bit stale but I don't suppose that matters.'

I was still a bit doubtful. I wanted to do it all *properly* but it couldn't be helped. When we got back to Cam's I carefully washed the dandelion leaf. It had been very hard to find. Cam eventually reached through the slats of someone's gate and picked a plant from their front garden.

'Um!' I said. 'Isn't that stealing?'

'It's weeding,' said Cam firmly. 'Dandelions are weeds.'

'If that *is* a dandelion.'

'Of course it is, Tracy.'

'What do you know about plants, Cam?'

'Look, I might not be Alan Titchmarsh, but I know my dandelions from my dock leaves. That is a dandelion, OK? So get chopping.'

I chopped the dandelion into little green specks, I crumbled the biscuits and spooned out the honey and sugar. Cam poured some wine into her prettiest pink wine glass. She lifted it absent-mindedly to her lips.

'Hey, hey, it's *my* potion!' I said.

'OK, OK,' said Cam, sighing. 'Go on then, shove the rest of the stuff in – though it seems a shame to muck up a perfectly good glass of wine.'

'This isn't a *drink*, Cam. It's a potion. *My* potion,' I said. 'Now, let me sprinkle and stir. You keep quiet. I have to concentrate.'

I concentrated like crazy, sprinkling in every little green dandelion speck and the ginger and the sugar and the honey, and then I stirred it vigorously with a spoon.

'Hey, gently with that glass!' said Cam.

'Shh! And don't listen to me, this is *private*,' I hissed. I took a deep breath. 'Please work, charm,' I muttered. 'Let me be with my Loved One on a Festive Occasion – i.e. this Christmas! I need her there to see me in *A Christmas Carol* and then I want her to stay so we have the best Christmas ever together.'

Then I raised the glass, stuck my chin in to reach the wrong side and took a gulp of wine without drawing breath. It tasted *disgusting*, but I swallowed it down determinedly, wishing and wishing to make it come true.

'Steady on, Tracy! Don't drink it all – you'll get drunk!' said Cam.

I didn't want to break the spell so I ignored her. I took another gulp and then spluttered and choked. The potion went up my nose and then snorted back out of it in a totally disgusting fashion. I gasped while Cam patted me on the back and mopped me with a tissue.

'Oh dear, have I mucked up the magic?' I wheezed.

'No, no, you absorbed the potion through extra orifices so I guess that makes it even more potent,' said Cam. 'Still, seriously, no more! Jenny would never forgive me if I took you back to the Home totally blotto.'

'Oh gosh, Cam, I think I *am* utterly totally sloshed out of my skull,' I slurred, reeling around, pretending to trip and stumble.

'Tracy!' said Cam, rushing to catch me.

'Only joking!' I giggled.

'Well, maybe I'd better have a swig too if it's as potent as that,' said Cam. She took the spoon and stirred it around herself, and then she mouthed something before she took a sip, drinking from the wrong side of the glass without drawing breath. Then she choked too, dribbling all down her chin.

It was my turn to clap her on the back.

'Hey, gently, Tracy!' Cam spluttered. 'Oh God. It tastes revolting. What a waste of wine.

Let's hope it jolly well works for both of us.'

'So who is *your* Loved One?' I said.

I wasn't too happy about this. As far as I knew Cam didn't have any Loved Ones, and that suited me just fine. I didn't want some bloke commandeering her on Saturdays and mucking up our special days together.

I knew what blokes could be like. That's how I started off in Care. My mum got this awful Monster Gorilla Boyfriend and he was horrible to me so I had to be taken away. I'd just like to see him try now. I was only little then. Well, I'm still quite little now but I am Incredibly Fierce and a Ferocious Fighter. Just ask Justine Bashed-To-A-Pulp Littlewood. If I encountered Monster Gorilla Boyfriend *now* I'd karate-chop him and then I'd kick him downstairs, out of the door, out of my life.

If Cam's anonymous Loved One started any funny business then he'd definitely get treated the same way. Beware the Beaker Boyfriend Deterrent!

'You haven't got a boyfriend, have you, Cam?' I asked her, as she fixed me a fruit smoothie to take away the terrible taste of the potion.

'A boyfriend?' said Cam, looking reassuringly surprised. 'Oh Tracy, don't *you* start. My mum always goes on at me whenever I see her.' She put on this piercing posh voice. *'Haven't you met any decent men yet, Camilla? Mind you, I'm not surprised no one's interested. Look at the state of you – that terrible short haircut and those wretched jeans!'*

Cam poured herself a glass of wine and took several sips. 'Oh dear. Shut me up whenever I get onto the subject of my mum.' She shuddered dramatically. 'OK, how's about trying a plateful of cinnamon toast?'

It was utterly yummy. I had six slices. I didn't get Cam's mum-phobia. I *love* talking about my mum. But then I've got the best and most beautiful movie-star actress for a mum. Maybe I wouldn't be anywhere near as keen if I had a snobby old bag for a mum like Cam.

I usually hate it when Cam takes me back to the Dumping Ground but I was quite cool about it this evening because I had Mega Things to Do. I raided Elaine's art therapy cupboard (I'm ace at picking locks) and helped myself to lots of bright pink tissue paper and the best thin white card and a set of halfway-decent felt-tip pens.

It wasn't really *stealing*. I was using them for dead artistic and extremely therapeutic purposes.

I shoved my art materials up my jumper and shuffled my way up to my room and then proceeded to be Creative.

I was still actively Creating when Jenny knocked on my door. She tried to come in but she couldn't, on account of the fact that I'd shoved my chair hard against it to repel all intruders.

'What are you up to in there, Tracy? Let me in!'

'Do you mind, Jenny? I'm working on something dead secret.'

'That's what I was afraid of! What are you doing? I want to see.'

'No, you mustn't look. I'm making Christmas presents,' I hissed.

'Ah!' said Jenny. 'Oh, Tracy, how lovely. I'm sorry, sweetheart, I'll leave you alone. But it's getting late. Switch your light out soon, pet.'

She went off down the corridor humming 'Jingle Bells', obviously thinking I was making *her* Christmas present. I'd have to get cracking now and make her something. Ditto Mike. Ditto Elaine. And ditto Cam, of course, though I would have liked to give her a proper present. Still, I had to have my priorities. Mum came first.

I wrapped the lipstick in pink tissue. Then I cut out a rectangle from the cardboard, drew a pair of smiley pink lips and carefully printed in tiny neat letters:

YOU WILL SMILE WITH SHINY LIPS
WHEN YOU SEE ME ACT SCROOGE
IN 'A CHRISTMAS CAROL',
7 PM WEDNESDAY 20 DECEMBER
AT KINGLEA JUNIOR SCHOOL!!!

I stuck the label on the first packet and then made three more. I drew two hands on the second label and printed:

YOU WILL CLAP TILL YOUR HANDS
ARE SORE WHEN YOU WATCH ME
AS SCROOGE IN 'A CHRISTMAS CAROL'
7 PM WEDNESDAY 20 DECEMBER
AT KINGLEA JUNIOR SCHOOL !!!

I stuck this label on the wrapped hand lotion.

On the *third* label I drew a big pulsing heart and printed:

YOUR HEART WILL THUMP WITH
PRIDE WHEN YOU SEE ME ACT SCROOGE
IN 'A CHRISTMAS CAROL'
7 PM WEDNESDAY 20 DECEMBER
AT KINGLEA JUNIOR SCHOOL !!!

Then I wrapped up the beautiful heart necklace, taking care not to twist the red ribbon, and stuck the label on the pink tissue parcel.

Three presents wrapped and labelled. Just one to go! It took the longest though, because I had to annotate the book of *A Christmas Carol*. I drew me dressed up as Scrooge inside the front cover, with a special bubble saying, *'Bah! Humbug!'* I drew me dressed up as Scrooge inside the back cover too, but this time I was taking a bow at the end of my performance. There were lots of clapping hands and speech bubbles saying HURRAY! and MAGNIFICENT! and WELL DONE, TRACY! and THE GREATEST PERFORMANCE EVER! and A TRUE STAR IS BORN!

I wrote on the title page:

You don't have to read all this book,
You just have to come and watch me act
Scrooge in 'A Christmas Carol', 7pm on
Wednesday 20 December at Kinglea
Junior School !!! I will dedicate my
performance to YOU, the best mum in
the whole world ever.
　　　All my love
　　　　　Tracy xxxxxxx

Then I wrapped *A Christmas Carol* and worked on the last label. I drew the book, scrunching up the title really small so it would fit, and underneath I printed:

THIS IS A GREAT BOOK AND IT'S BEEN TURNED INTO A GREAT PLAY AND THE GREATEST PART IS SCROOGE AND I AM PLAYING HIM (7PM ON WEDNESDAY 20 DECEMBER AT KINGLEA JUNIOR SCHOOL) SO PLEASE PLEASE PLEASE COME AND WATCH ME! ALL MY LOVE Tracy XXXXXXXX

Then I sat for a long time holding all four pink parcels on my lap, imagining my mum opening them and putting on her lipstick, rubbing in her hand lotion, fastening the heart necklace, looking at the messages in the book. I imagined her jumping in her car and driving directly to see her superstar daughter. She'd be so proud of me she'd never ever want to go away without me.

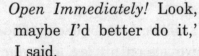

The next morning I cornered Jenny in her office and asked if she had a big Jiffy bag so I could send my presents to my mum.

'It's a little bit early to send your Christmas presents, isn't it, Tracy?' Jenny said.

'No, no, these are *before* Christmas presents,' I said. 'We have to send them off first thing on Monday morning. First class.'

'OK. First thing, first class. I suppose *I'm* paying the postage?' said Jenny.

'Yes, and can you write on the Jiffy bag *Urgent! Open Immediately!* Look, maybe *I'd* better do it,' I said.

'I think I can manage that, Tracy,' said Jenny.

'You are sure you've got my mum's right address?' I asked anxiously.

They don't let me have

it now on account of the fact that I tried to run away to find her. They won't let me have her phone number either. It is bitterly unfair, seeing as she's *my* mother. I have had major mega strops about it, but they won't give in.

'Don't worry, Tracy, I've got your mum's address,' said Jenny.

'It's just that it's ultra important. I need her to come and see me in the school play,' I said.

'I'm so glad you've been picked for the play, Tracy. You will take it seriously, won't you? No messing around or you'll spoil it for everyone.'

'Of course I'm taking it seriously, Jenny,' I said, insulted.

I was taking it very very very seriously – unlike *some* people. We had a play rehearsal every lunch time and half the kids mucked about and ate their sandwiches as they mumbled their lines. The carol singers sang off-key and the extra ghosts whimpered rather than wailed and the dancers kept bumping into each other and Weedy Peter kept forgetting his lines. He even forgot which was his lame leg, limping first on his left leg and then on his right.

'You are just so totally useless, Peter. How can you *possibly* keep forgetting "God bless us every one"?' said Justine Big-Mouth Littlewood. She seized hold of him and made like she was peering into his ear. 'Yes, just as I thought. You've not got any brain at all. It's just empty space inside your niddy-noddy head.'

I was thinking on similar lines myself, but when I saw poor Peter's face crumple I felt furious with her.

'You leave Peter alone, Justine Great-Big-Bully Littlewood. He's doing just fine – unlike you! I've never seen such a pathetic ghost in all my life. You're meant to be spooky but you couldn't scare so much as a sausage.'

Miss Simpkins clapped her hands. 'Hey, hey, girls! Calm down now. Concentrate on the play,' she said. 'Justine, you could put a little more *effort* into your Marley portrayal. Tracy, maybe you could try a little *less*. You're a splendid Scrooge but you don't need to furrow your brow and scowl *quite* so ferociously, and I think spitting at people when you say

"Bah! Humbug!" is a little too emphatic, plus I don't think the caretaker would approve of you dribbling all over the stage.'

'I'm simply getting under the skin of my character, Miss Simpkins,' I said.

She wasn't listening. She was busy shepherding the spare ghosts into a haunting formation.

'Yeah, you get under everyone's skin, Tracy Beaker,' hissed Justine Make-No-Effort-At-All Littlewood. 'You're like a big pus-y pimple.'

Louise giggled. 'Watch out or we'll squeeze you!' she said.

I gave her a shove. She shoved me back. Justine shoved too, harder. I was a bit off balance, hunched up in crabbed Scrooge mode. I ended up on my bottom.

They laughed. I tried not to cry because it hurt so much. Not that I ever cry, of course.

But sudden shocks to my system occasionally bring on an attack of my hay fever. It wasn't just bumping my bum. It was the fact that Louise was being so horrible. I was used to Justine Mean-Mouth Littlewood being foul to me, but it was so unfair that Louise was ganging up with her against me.

Louise had always been *my* friend. Now I didn't have any friend at all apart from Weedy Peter, and he barely counted.

'She's *crying*! You baby!' said Justine Mockingbird-Big-Beak Littlewood.

'Why don't you fight back, Tracy?' said Louise, looking uncomfortable.

'She's lost her bottle,' said Justine Hateful-Pig Littlewood. 'Boo-hoo, boo-hoo, baby! Does little diddums wants her mumsy to kiss it better? Only dream on, diddums, cause Mumsy isn't ever ever ever going to come.'

'I'll show you if I've lost my bottle,' I said, struggling to my feet.

I went *push punch whack kick!* Justine reeled backwards, her big nose all bloody after intimate contact with my fist.

At that precise moment Mrs Darlow the headteacher came through the swing doors to see how the Christmas play was progressing. For a split second we were all stopped in our tracks, as if we'd been Paused. Then we were Fast Forwarded into alarming and ear-splitting action.

Justine started screaming. Louise did too, though I didn't even touch her. Peter started wailing. Some of the little kid dancers and carol singers started whimpering. Miss Simpkins looked like she wanted to burst into tears too.

She rushed over to Justine and picked her up and peered at her bloody nose.

Mrs Darlow marched over to me, snorting through *her* nose. 'Tracy Beaker, how dare you attack another pupil! How many times have I got to tell you that I will *not* have fighting in my school?'

'But Mrs Darlow, it wasn't exactly my fault. I didn't start it,' I protested.

I wasn't going to tell tales on Justine Scarlet-Fountain-For-A-Nose Littlewood, but I felt I needed to indicate that I'd been Severely Provoked.

Mrs Darlow clapped her hands at me to shut me up. 'In my experience it's *always* your fault, Tracy Beaker,' she said.

This was profoundly unfair. I wished I had enough bottle left to *push punch whack kick* Mrs Darlow. I wanted to see her sprawling on her back, arms and legs flung out, skirts up, knickers showing.

It was such a bizarre image that I couldn't help sniggering. This was fatal.

'How *dare* you act as if this is a laughing matter! I'm tired of your temper tantrums. You're going to have to learn your lesson once and for all. You will not take part in the school play this Christmas!'

'But I have to be in the play, Mrs Darlow. I'm Scrooge. I'm the main part!'

'Not any more,' said Mrs Darlow.

'But my mum's coming to see me!' I said. 'I've written and told her all about it and she's coming specially.'

'I can't help that, Tracy Beaker. You're not taking part in the school play and that's that.'

I lost it then. Totally utterly out-of-it lost it. I opened my mouth and started yelling. Miss Simpkins put her arm round me but I shook her off. Peter clasped my hand but I wrenched it free. I lay down, shut my eyes and shrieked. And shrieked and shrieked and shrieked.

Eventually someone hoicked me up and carted me off to the sickroom. I opened my eyes momentarily. Justine Hate-Her-Guts Littlewood was sitting on a chair with her head back, a big wodge of tissues clutched to her bleeding nose. I closed my eyes and carried on shrieking.

I heard murmurings and mutterings. When I next opened my eyes I couldn't see Justine. I didn't know what had happened to her. I didn't care. I wished everyone in the whole world would disappear. Everyone except my mum.

I thought about Mum getting her Christmas presents, looking at her copy of *A Christmas Carol*, dressing up in her prettiest clothes and tying her heart necklace round her neck, rubbing her hand lotion on her slim fingers and applying her new lipstick into a shiny pink smile. I saw her arriving at the school on 20 December, sitting right at the front ready to watch me act. Only I wouldn't be in it. I wouldn't be in it. I wouldn't be in it.

I shrieked some more, even though my throat ached and my head thumped and I was burning hot and wet with sweat. I knew it was time to stop howling but I couldn't. I tried clamping my mouth shut but the shrieks built up inside and then came shouting out louder than ever. It was so scary that I started shaking. I couldn't stop. I was cursed like a creature in a fairy tale, condemned to scream for all eternity.

Then I felt new hands on my shoulders and Jenny's familiar firm voice.

'Easy, Tracy. It's OK. I'm here now. They sent for me. Now stop the noise.'

'I . . . can't!' I shrieked.

'Yes, you can. Take deep breaths. In. And now out. That's the ticket. Don't worry, I've got you. You're stopping now, see?'

I clung to Jenny like a little toddler. She knelt down and rocked me while I nuzzled into her shoulder.

'OK now?' she said eventually.

'No!' I paused. I opened my eyes and blinked hard, peering around the room.

'Justine?' I whispered.

'She's been taken to hospital,' said Jenny, sighing.

'Oh!'

I started shaking again. What had I *done*? I'd only bopped her on the nose. I'd done that several times before and she'd never been hurt enough to go to *hospital*. What if I'd hit her so hard her entire nose had burst and now she just had a big bloody blob in the middle of her face? What if her whole *head* had exploded and now they were trying to stitch all the bits back together again?

I hated Justine and I always would but I didn't want her to be seriously *hurt*. What if she didn't get better? What if she bled so much she died? I pictured her lying there limp and white in hospital, doctors and nurses and Louise and Justine's dad gathered round her bedside.

I saw her funeral, all the Dumping Ground kids trailing along in black behind her hearse. I saw Louise weeping, carrying a huge wreath.

I tried to tell her I was sorry, but she turned on me and told me I was a murderer. Everyone started murmuring the awful word – *Murderer, murderer, Tracy Beaker is a murderer* – and then I heard sirens and a whole squad of police cars arrived and the police leaped out and ran towards me brandishing their truncheons and I started to run in terror, screaming—

'Tracy! Don't start again,' said Jenny. 'I'm sure Justine is OK. Well, she's not, her poor nose bled horribly and you are going to be severely punished for it, my girl, but I don't think there's any long-term harm. Mrs Darlow is worried you might have broken Justine's nose, but I think she's over-reacting a little. Now, I'm going to take you back home. You need to calm down in the Quiet Room. Then we'll talk things over and see what we can do.'

I let her steer me out of the room and down the corridor. The bell had gone for play time and there were hordes of kids milling up and down, staring staring staring.

'Look at Tracy Beaker!'

'What's the matter with Tracy Beaker?'

'Hey, someone said she's had this ginormous tantrum and screamed her head off.'

'She screamed all sorts of bad words at Mrs Darlow!'

'She attacked Justine Littlewood and she's been rushed to hospital in an ambulance!'

'She punched Mrs Darlow right on the nose!'

'She's not allowed to be in the school play any more!'

I moaned and snorted and sniffled. Jenny gave me a gentle push past them all, out through the doors and across the playground. I started shivering and shaking, knuckling my eyes to try to dry them up.

I hated it that so many of them had seen me in a state. It's different at the Dumping Ground. Everyone understands that looked-after kids are a bit like fireworks with very short fuses. Beware matches! Some of us just do a little fizz and whizz when someone sets them off. Weedy Peter's mini-tantrums are like little kiddy sparklers. Some of us explode loudly like bangers, but it's all over quickly without too much show. And *some* of us are like mega rockets and we soar and swoop and explode into a million stars. No prizes for guessing which firework *I* fit.

They don't get it at school. They especially don't get me. I didn't mind them knowing I'd socked Justine. I rather liked it that they thought I'd punched Mrs Darlow. But I hated them all seeing me in such a state, all blood, sweat and tears. I didn't mind the blood, I didn't mind the sweat, but Tracy Beaker doesn't cry. Ever. Not publicly, anyway.

The minivan was a very private place. And so is the Quiet Room. And my bedroom. Jenny said I could come down to tea but I didn't fancy the idea.

Mike brought a tray upstairs to my room.

'Hey, Tracy. I know you're in disgrace, but I wouldn't want you to miss out on spag bol, and it's particularly tasty tonight.'

He thrust the tray under my nose. My nostrils prickled with the rich savoury smell, but I turned my head away.

'I'm not really hungry, Mike,' I said.

'Miss Fussy-Gussy. I've slaved at the stove for hours so the least you can do is try a mouthful,' said Mike, balancing the tray on my lap and twisting spaghetti round and round the fork.

'Come on, sweetie. Here's an aeroplane – *wheee* through the air and *in* it swoops,' he said, guying the way he fed the very little kids in the Dumping Ground.

I kept my lips clamped. I didn't even smile at him. I didn't feel in the mood for jokes (even sweet ones) or food (though spag bol was a special favourite).

'Come on, Tracy. Even Justine hasn't lost her appetite, yet she's the girl with the poorly nose.'

'Is she back from the hospital?' I said.

'Yep. Poor, poor Justine,' said Mike.

'Is her nose really broken?' I whispered.

'Broken right *off*,' said Mike – but then he saw my expression. '*Joke*, Tracy. It's fine. You just gave her a little nosebleed. But Jenny and I have got to put our heads together and find some suitable means of punishment. You've got to learn to handle your temper, Tracy, especially at school. Jenny and I are sick of apologizing to old Dragon Darlow. She's always been a tad wary of all our kids – you in particular, Ms Biff and Bash Beaker. Every time you throw a wobbly at school you're confirming all her prejudices.'

'You can punish me any way you want,' I said wanly. 'You can beat me and starve me and lock me in the cupboard.'

'There's not much point,' said Mike. 'If I tried to beat you I'm sure you'd beat me right back. You're already starving yourself going without your spag bol. And there's no point shutting you in the art cupboard because I have a shrewd suspicion you know how to pick that lock already. No, I think we'll have to come up with something more to the point.'

'I told you, Mike, I don't care. Mrs Darlow's punished me already. She won't let me be Scrooge any more and my mum won't get to see me act,' I said.

Some drops of water dribbled down my face and splashed into the plate of spaghetti on my lap.

'I know how tough that is, Tracy,' Mike said, and he gave me a little hug. 'I know how hard you've worked on your part, and I'm sure you'd have been the Scroogiest Scrooge ever. I think we both know that we can't take it for granted that your mum can come to see you – but if she *did* just happen to be there she'd be so proud of you, sweetheart. All the kids think Mrs Darlow's being very unfair. They say the play won't be the same without you, Tracy.'

'Who are you trying to kid, Mike?' I said wearily, but I reached out and tried a very small forkful of spaghetti. It was still hot and surprisingly tasty.

'I mean it, Tracy. Little Peter's absolutely beside himself. He's thinking of starting up some petition.'

'Ah. Sweet,' I said, trying another forkful. 'Still, I bet Louise and

Justine are thrilled to bits that I'm out of the play.'

'Well, you're wrong then, chum. I know you three aren't the best of mates nowadays, but Louise seems quite uncomfortable about the situation. I think she feels she and Justine might just have provoked your sudden savage attack.'

'Really?' I said, starting to scoop up my spag bol enthusiastically. 'What about Justine? What does she say?'

'Well, she's probably the only one of the kids who isn't as yet a signed-up member of the Justice for Tracy Fan Club. That's hardly surprising as her poor nose is still swollen and sore.'

'Oh dear,' I said insincerely.

Mike ruffled my curls. 'You're a bad bad girl, little Beaker. We're going to have to channel all that aggression somehow.' That sounded ominous.

I was right to be suspicious. The next morning Jenny and Mike cornered me as I came downstairs, head held high, determined to show everyone I was absolutely fine now, so long as everyone kept their gob shut about mums and plays and headteachers.

I held my head a little too high, so I couldn't see where I was going. Some stupid little kid had set a small herd of plastic dinosaurs to graze on the carpet at the foot of the stairs. I skidded and very nearly went bonk on my bum again, but this time my natural grace and agility enabled me to keep my footing – just.

'Why don't you make the kids clear up all their little plastic whatsits?' I demanded.

'Good point, Tracy,' said Mike.

'Maybe you'll help us, Tracy,' said Jenny. 'It will make your job easier.'

I paused. I eyed them suspiciously. 'What job?'

'We've thought of an excellent way to channel your aggression,' said Mike.

'Don't think of this as a punishment, Tracy. It's a positive way to make this a happy, clean and tidy home,' said Jenny.

The words *clean* and *tidy* reverberated ominously, scouring my ears.

'Hey, you're not plotting that I'm going to be,

152

like, your *cleaning lady*?' I said.

'Quick off the mark as always, Tracy Beaker,' said Mike.

'We feel you'll do an excellent job,' said Jenny.

'You can't force me! There's a law against child labour!' I protested.

'We're not employing you, Tracy. We're simply helping you manage your anger in a practical fashion.'

'What sort of practical?'

'You just have to tidy and dust and vacuum and clean the bathrooms and give the kitchen floor a quick scrub.'

I thought quickly. 'So how much are you going to pay me?'

'Ah. Well, we thought you would want to do this first week as a trial run. If you want a permanent position after that I'm sure we could start financial negotiations,' said Jenny. 'Now, run and have your breakfast or you'll be late for school.'

'But—'

'No buts, Tracy,' said Mike firmly.

I know when it's a waste of Beaker breath pursuing a point. I stamped into the kitchen and sat down at the table. I shook cornflakes into a bowl so violently that they sprayed out onto the table. I poured milk so fiercely that it gushed like Niagara Falls and overflowed my bowl.

They were all staring at me warily. Even Justine looked a little anxious. She kept rubbing her nose.

'Are you OK, Tracy?' Peter squeaked.

'Do I *seem* OK?' I snapped, slamming my spoon down.

Peter jumped and the juice in his cup spilled onto the table.

'For heaven's sake, watch what you're doing!' I said, though I'd actually made much more mess myself. 'I'm the poor cleaning lady now. I've got to mop up after all you lot, so watch out, do you hear me?'

'I should think the people right at the end of the road can hear you,' said Louise. 'And don't pick on poor little Peter. He's started up a petition on your behalf: "Please let Tracy Beaker play Scrooge". He's going to get everyone to sign it.'

'Shh, Louise. It's a secret,' said Peter, blushing.

'Yes, like Mrs Darlow is going to be heavily influenced by Peter's pathetic petition,' I said.

Then I saw his little face. Crumple time again. I felt so mean I couldn't bear it, but I couldn't say anything in front of the others. I just gobbled down my breakfast and then cleared off back to my room to collect my school bag and stuff. I listened out for Peter. I caught him scuttling back from the bathroom, toothpaste round his mouth.

'Hey, Peter!' I hissed.

He jumped again, his tongue nervously licking the white foam off his lips.

'Come in my room a second,' I commanded.

Peter caught his breath. He backed into my bedroom obediently and stood with his back against my Vampire Bat poster, his fists clenched, as if he was facing a firing squad.

'It's OK, Peter,' I said. 'I'm not going to beat you up.'

'I'm sorry if I annoyed you with my petition idea. I know it's a bit silly and maybe pointless but I felt so bad about you not being in the play any more and I just wanted to do something.'

'I was just being a bad-tempered pig at breakfast. I didn't mean to get cross with you, Pete. I think your petition's a lovely idea. Nobody's ever put me in a petition before. I still don't see that it will *achieve* anything, but I think it's ever so sweet of you. You're a very special friend. Thank you. Ever so much.'

Peter still didn't move but he went raspberry-red and blinked at me rapidly.

'Oh, Tracy,' he said.

I gave him a little pat on the head. He tried to

give me a big hug but I wasn't prepared to go *that* far.

'Hey, watch out, you're wiping toothpaste all over me. Come on, we'll be late for school.'

'So can I carry on with my petition?'

'Feel free. Though I doubt you'll get many people to sign it on account of the fact that I'm not the most popular girl in the school. Um . . . have the kids here *really* signed it?'

'Yes, all of them. Well, Justine hasn't quite managed to get round to it yet, but I'll keep badgering her.'

'Oh, Peter, you couldn't badger anyone!'

'You wait and see, Tracy. I'll get the whole school to sign the petition. You *have* to be in the play. You're totally brilliant at acting Scrooge.'

'You're wasting your time, Pete, but thanks anyway,' I said. 'It's great that you've got such faith in my acting abilities. Tell you what, when I'm grown up and a famous movie star just like my mum, I'll let you be my agent, OK?'

This perked him up no end but it had the opposite effect on me. Just mentioning my mum made me want to start howling again. But I had to go to school and control all emotion. Yesterday I'd screamed and shrieked. Today I was going to be calm and in control to show everyone that Tracy Beaker is One Tough Cookie, able to cope with incredible public humiliation without turning a hair.

It wasn't as easy as that. I jumped out of the Dumping Ground minivan and walked into school as nonchalantly as possible, but everyone in the playground turned and stared and pointed at me. A group of little kids actually stood round me in a circle as if they could turn me on like a television and watch *The Tracy Beaker Freak Show*.

The kids staring at me wasn't the worse part. It was the teachers. They were crazily *kind* to me. Miss Brown actually hovered by my desk when she was collecting up maths homework and said softly, 'How are you doing, Tracy?'

Miss Brown

'Not too good, Miss Brown,' I muttered.

'I don't suppose you managed to do your maths homework last night?'

'I was kind of Otherwise Engaged,' I said.

'Oh well. Not to worry. You can do it in your lunch hour.'

'OK, I've got all the time in the world in my lunch hour now,' I said, sighing heavily.

The lunch hour was dreadful. Peter and Louise and Justine and all the other kids in *A Christmas Carol* rushed off to the hall to rehearse . . . without me.

I stayed in the classroom all by myself and did my maths homework. The inky numbers on my page kept blurring and blotching, as if they were being rained on. I used up two tissues and my sleeve mopping up.

I whizzed along to the cloakroom just before

the start of afternoon school to splash cold water on my face – and bumped into Miss Simpkins. She had Gloria Taylor, Emily Lawson and Amy Jellicoe with her. They were all looking up at her hopefully, eyes huge like puppies in Battersea Dogs Home, going, *Pick me, Miss Simpkins*.

'Oh, Tracy,' said Miss Simpkins. She waved her hand at Gloria and Emily and Amy. 'Run along, girls. I'll let you know tomorrow,' she said.

They each gave me a pitying glance and then ran off obediently.

'They've been auditioning for Scrooge, haven't they?' I said flatly.

'Yes, they have,' said Miss Simpkins. She lowered her voice to a whisper. 'And they all tried their best, but strictly between you and me, Tracy, they're rubbish compared to you.'

'So which one are you going to pick, Miss Simpkins?'

'I don't know,' she said, sighing. 'It's such a

big part and there's hardly any time left to learn it. Gloria's the only girl who could learn it all by heart, but she runs through it like a railway station announcer, with no expression whatsoever. Emily can at least act a little, but she can't remember two consecutive lines so she'd have to have the script in her hands the whole time and that would spoil things.'

'So are you going to choose Amy for Scrooge?'

'Amy is so sweet and soft and shy she can barely make herself heard and she can't act bad-tempered to save her life. She just doesn't *convince* as Scrooge.'

'Whereas I can act bad-tempered till the cows come home,' I said.

'Yes! You were my magnificent Scrooge,' she said, sighing.

'Until Mrs Darlow spoiled everything,' I said.

'No, Tracy. Until *you* spoiled everything,' said Miss Simpkins. 'Although I know you were severely provoked. I've tried explaining the circumstances to Mrs Darlow – in vain, I'm sorry to say.'

'Well. Thank you, Miss Simpkins,' I said. 'I'm sorry I mucked it all up.'

'It seems a shame you've got to pay so dearly

for it,' said Miss Simpkins.

'You don't know the half of it,' I said darkly. 'I'm paying for it with knobs on, even back at the Home. I'm acting as an unpaid skivvy clearing up after all the kids. Isn't that unbelievably unfair? I think you should report them to the NSPCC, OK?'

'I'll think about it,' said Miss Simpkins, but she was struggling hard not to laugh.

I *certainly* didn't feel like laughing when I came home utterly exhausted from school to have Jenny hand me the hoover and Mike thrust the mop and bucket at me.

I'd been secretly hoping that this was one big bluff. I was outraged to realize they really meant to go through with it.

'Let me have my tea first, for pity's sake,' I said.

I took my time munching my banana wholemeal sandwich and my handful of nuts and my orange and my apple juice. (Oh for the days of unhealthy eating when we wolfed down crisps and chocolate and cakes and Coke.) Then I stomped off to my room to change out of my school uniform and put on my oldest jeans and faded T-shirt.

I stopped to look at the postcard from Mum on my notice board. I suddenly felt so sad I had to lie on my bed with my head under my pillow just in case anyone overheard my sudden attack of hay fever. I was still feeling sniffly when I trailed down the stairs, sighing considerably. No one was around to hear me. The other kids all seemed to be whispering together in the kitchen. It was all right for *some* Ugly People. Poor little Cinderella Beaker had to stay home and tackle all the chores.

I picked up the hoover, switched it on and started shoving it backwards and forwards across the hall. It was so heavy, so clumsy, so awkward. My arms were aching and my back hurt from bending over already and yet I'd only done one weeny patch of carpet. I had the whole huge Dumping Ground to render spotless. I banged the hoover violently into the skirting board and gave it a kick. I was only wearing soft shoes. It hurt *horribly*. I switched the hateful hoover off and doubled up, nursing my poor stubbed toes.

I heard more whisperings and gigglings.

'Shut up, you lot!' I snarled.

Peter popped his head round the kitchen door. 'Tracy, are you *OK*?'

'I'm absolutely in the pink,' I said sarcastically. 'In the rose-pink, salmon-pink, petunia-pink – *not*. How do you think I feel, knowing I've got the tremendous task of cleaning up the Dumping Ground single-handed?'

'Not *quite* single-handed,' said Peter. 'Come on, gang!'

All the kids suddenly sprang out of the kitchen into the hall. Peter stood in front, jersey sleeves rolled up his puny little arms, a tea towel tied round his waist like a pinny. They were all clutching dusters and mops and brushes and pans. Louise was there, her long hair tied up in a scarf. Justine sloped out last, wearing Mike's stripy cooking apron and wielding a scrubbing brush.

'We're all going to do the cleaning,' said Peter. 'It seemed so horribly mean that you had to do it all, so we're helping out. It'll be fun!'

'Not *my* idea of fun, you little runt,' said Justine, juggling her scrubbing brush.

Louise caught it and held onto it. 'It was just as much our fault as yours, Tracy,' she said. 'We *all* got mad, so Peter's right, we should all channel our aggression into housework.'

'So OK, troops, let's get cracking!' Peter said. He looked at me. 'OK, Tracy?'

For once I was totally speechless. I just nodded very hard and blinked very hard and hoped very hard that I wouldn't utterly disgrace myself and howl. We let funny little Peter order us around, telling each of us what to do, because it was easier than us big ones arguing about it. We put radios playing the loudest rock and rap music in every corner of the Dumping Ground and then set to with a vengeance.

Elaine the Pain came calling halfway through. She cowered backwards, covering her ears, but when Jenny and Mike explained (having to bellow a bit), she clapped her hands excitedly and went prancing around congratulating everyone on their team spirit.

'It reflects the very essence of Christmas, loving and sharing and caring,' she said, jamming her reindeer antlers on her head and rushing around giving everyone a little pat on the back.

It's a wonder Elaine Ridiculous Reindeer Pain didn't make them think: *What on earth am I doing scrubbing away when I could be watching the telly or playing on my Xbox or simply lounging on my bed picking my nose because I definitely don't love Tracy Beaker and I don't care tuppence about her and I certainly don't want to share her stupid punishment.* But somehow they took no notice and carried on dusting and scrubbing and scouring and hoovering. I felt as if all the dirty grubby grimy greasy little bits of me were getting a clean and polish too. Maybe they did like me just a little bit after all.

I still had some stuff left over from my raid on the art cupboard. That night I laboured long and hard over a big card. I drew the Dumping Ground and all of us guys outside, armed with dusters and brushes and mops. I even drew Justine properly, though it was very tempting to cross her eyes and scribble little bogeys hanging from her nose. I put me in the centre with a big beaming smile. I drew little rays of sunshine all round my picture and

then I printed at the top in dead artistic rainbow
lettering:

I crept downstairs and stuck it on the table
so that everyone would see it at breakfast time.
I snaffled half a packet of cornflakes and an
orange so I could have breakfast in my room. I
didn't want to be hanging around when they
saw the card. It would be *way* too embarrassing.
I wasn't used to acting all mushy and saying
thank you. I'd have to watch it. I was used to

being the toughest kid on the block. It would be fatal to soften up now.

I tried hard to be my normal fierce and feisty self at school. I summoned up all my energy to cheek the teachers and argue with the kids but it was hard work. I found myself sharing my chocolate bar with Peter in the playground and picking up some little kid who'd fallen over and kicking someone's ball straight back to them, acting like Ms Goody-Goody Two Trainers instead of the Tough and Terrible Tracy Beaker,

When everyone went to rehearse *A Christmas Carol* I wondered which of the Three Stooges Miss Simpkins had picked as Scrooge. I couldn't help being glad that they were all pretty useless.

Halfway through the first lesson in the afternoon Mrs Darlow sent for me.

'Oh, Tracy,' said Miss Brown sorrowfully. 'What have you been up to *now*?'

'Nothing, Miss Brown!' I said. 'I've been a positive angel all day.'

Miss Brown didn't look as if she believed me. I couldn't really blame her. She wasn't to know I was this new squeaky-clean sweet-as-honey Beaker.

I plodded along to Mrs Darlow's study, wondering if she was going to blame me for someone else's misdemeanour. Maybe she'd think *I'd* written the very very rude rhyme in the girls' toilets. Maybe she'd think *I'd* superglued some teacher's chair. Maybe she'd think *I'd* climbed up the drainpipe after a lost ball and pulled the pipe right off the wall in the process. I *had* done all these things in the past, but not *recently*.

Still, I would doubtless be blamed. I sighed wearily and knocked on Mrs Darlow's door, deciding that there was no point protesting my total innocence to such a grim and unforgiving woman. She was doubtless preparing to Punish Tracy Beaker Severely. I saw her selecting her whippiest whip, her thumb crunchers, her nose tweakers, clearing her desk of superfluous paperwork so she could stretch me across it as if I was on a torture rack. I'd crawl out of school lashed into bloody stripes, thumbs mangled, nose pulled past my chin, stretched out and out and out like elastic.

Mrs Darlow was wearing her severest black trouser suit. She sat at her desk, her chin in her hands, frowning at me over the top of her glasses.

'Come and sit down, Tracy Beaker,' she said.

She always says my name in full, though there isn't another Tracy in the whole school.

'How are you today?' she enquired.

'Not especially happy, Mrs Darlow,' I said.

'Neither am I, Tracy Beaker, neither am I,' she said. She took hold of a large wad of paper scribbled all over with lots of names. 'Do you know what this is?'

I paused. I had a feeling that it wasn't the time to say 'pieces of paper'.

'I don't know, Mrs Darlow' seemed a safer bet. I truly didn't know. The handwriting wasn't mine. It was all different writing, some neat, some scrawly, in black, blue, red – all the colours of the rainbow.

'This is a petition to reinstate you as Scrooge in the school play,' said Mrs Darlow.

'Oh goodness! Peter's petition!' I said.

'Are you sure you didn't put him up to it, Tracy Beaker?'

'Absolutely not!' I said. 'But he's got heaps and heaps of signatures!'

'Yes, he has. Though I've scrutinized every page, and some of the signatures are duplicated – and I'm not sure Mickey Mouse, Homer Simpson, Robbie Williams and Beyoncé are actually pupils at this school.'

My mouth twitched. I was scared I was going to get the giggles, and yet my eyes were pricking as if I had a bout of hay fever coming on. All those signatures! I thought of Peter going round and round and round the whole school with his petition and all those kids signing away, wanting *me* in the play.

'Peter's obviously a very kind friend,' said Mrs Darlow.

'Yes, he is,' I said humbly.

'I'm rather impressed by his initiative and perseverance. When he delivered the petition this morning he was trembling all over, but he still made his own personal impassioned plea. He stated – accurately – that there is no other girl remotely like you, Tracy Beaker.'

I smiled.

'He meant it as a compliment. I didn't,' said Mrs Darlow. 'I felt very sorry for poor Peter when I told him that it was highly unlikely I would change my mind, even though I was very impressed by his petition.'

'Oh,' I said, slumping in my chair.

'Then I had a visit from Miss Simpkins at lunch time. She's already tried to plead your cause, Tracy Beaker. She's told me that your appalling assault wasn't entirely unprovoked. However, I've explained to her that I can never condone violent behaviour, no matter what the circumstances.'

I sighed and slumped further down the chair.

'However . . .' said Mrs Darlow.

I stiffened.

'Miss Simpkins invited me along to rehearsals. The play itself is progressing perfectly. Everyone's worked very hard.

I watched Gloria and Emily and Amy play Scrooge, one after the other. They tried extremely hard. In fact I awarded them five team points each for endeavour. Unfortunately though, none of the girls is a born actress, and although they tried their best I could see that their performances were a little . . . lacking.'

I clenched my fists.

'Miss Simpkins stressed that *your* performance as Scrooge was extraordinary, Tracy Beaker. I am very aware that this is a *public* performance in front of all the parents.'

'My mum's coming,' I whispered.

'It is a showcase event, and therefore I want everything to be perfect. I don't want all that hard work and effort to be wasted. I've decided to reinstate you, Tracy Beaker. You may play Scrooge after all.'

'Oh, Mrs Darlow! You are a total *angel*!' I said, sitting bolt upright and clapping my hands.

'I'm not sure you're going to

think me so totally angelic by the time I've finished, Tracy Beaker. I said violent behaviour can never be condoned. You must still be severely punished in some other way.'

'*Any* way, Mrs Darlow. Be as inventive as you like. Whips, thumbscrews, nose tweakers, the rack. Whatever.'

'I think I'll select a more mundane punishment, Tracy Beaker, though the nose tweaker sounds tempting,' said Mrs Darlow. 'And appropriate in the circumstances, as you hit poor Justine on *her* nose. However, I'm not sure the school's petty cash can quite cover an instrument of torture. We are already well stocked with cleaning implements so we will stick with those.'

'Cleaning implements, Mrs Darlow?' I said. 'Oh no! I've already had to clean the entire Dumping Ground – I mean, the Home. You're not asking me to clean the whole *school*?'

'As if I'd ask you to do that!' said Mrs Darlow. 'I might not be angelic, but I am reasonable. I think I shall just ask you to clean the hall floor. If we're having all these guests then we can't have the setting looking downright scruffy. I'd like you to stay after school for half an hour every evening and polish up the parquet. It will not only enhance the look of the school, it will also act as a channel for your aggression.'

'My aggression's already been thoroughly channelled, Mrs Darlow,' I said. 'But all right, I will. I'll polish the whole hall until we can all see straight up our skirts, just so long as my mum will be able to see me act Scrooge.'

I don't know if you've ever done any serious polishing? Your hand hurts, your arms ache, your neck twinges, your back's all bent, your knees get rubbed raw, even your toes get scrunched up and sore. Think of the size of a school hall. Think of me.

Long long long did I labour. Dear old Peter and some of the other kids tried to sneak into the hall to help me out, but Mrs Darlow didn't appreciate this kind of caring and sharing teamwork.

'It's Tracy Beaker's punishment, not yours. I want her to labour on her own!' she said.

So labour I did, but I kept a copy of the play in front of me as I polished. I went over and over my lines in my head.

It was actually quite a good way of learning them, rubbing a long line of shiny wood while muttering a long line of Scrooge-speak. Every time I dipped my cloth into the polish I went, 'Bah! Humbug!' Whenever I finished a whole section I said Tiny Tim's 'God bless us, every one.' By the time I'd polished the entire hall floor I not only knew my lines, I knew everyone else's too.

I couldn't *wait* till Wednesday, the day of our performance. I was in a fever of impatience, positively burning up all over, so much so that Jenny caught hold of me at breakfast and felt my forehead.

'Are you feeling OK, Tracy? You're very flushed.'

'Oh, Tracy, you're not ill, are you?' said Peter. He shivered. '*I* feel ill. I hardly slept last night and when I did I kept dreaming I was standing on the stage all alone and people kept shouting rude things to me. I wish wish wish I didn't have to act. I'm simply dreading tonight. What if I forget what to say?'

'You'll be fine, Pete. You won't forget. And if you *do*, just look at me and I'll whisper them for you,' I said.

'Yeah, the one and only Big-mouth Beaker,' sneered Justine.

She didn't look too well herself. She was very pale, with dark circles under her eyes.

'You look like Marley's Ghost already, without bothering with make-up,' I said. 'Getting worried you'll be rubbish?'

'Absolutely *not*.' Justine paused. 'What about you, Tracy? Are you getting worried? Worried your mum might not turn up to watch you? Ha, that's a laugh. Your mum's as rarely sighted as the Abominable Snowman.'

There was a sudden silence. Everyone stopped chomping their cornflakes.

'Justine, button that lip!' said Mike.

'Tracy, don't start anything!' said Jenny.

I wasn't going to show Justine Spooky-Spectre Littlewood she could rattle me. I smiled at her, teeth clenched. I felt my tummy clenching too, into a tight little ball. Mum *would* come, wouldn't she?

She'd surely want to see me act the leading part in our school play. She'd want to sit right in the middle, surrounded by happy clapping parents, all of them saying, 'That Tracy Beaker's a great little actress. I wonder where she gets that from?' Then they'd look round and spot Mum, all glamorous and gorgeous, and go, '*She* must be Tracy's mum. Oh my goodness, of *course*! She's the movie star Carly Beaker!'

She'd be there tonight, clutching her copy of *A Christmas Carol*, wearing her lipstick and her hand cream and her heart necklace. She'd *have* to come when I'd tried so hard with her presents. She'd want to give me a big hug and kiss and clap till her hands smarted, and then she'd sweep me off for ever because she was so proud of me.

'Dream on, Tracy,' Justine Poison-Mouth Littlewood muttered.

The fist inside my tummy squeezed tighter. *Was* it all a daydream? Was I really just kidding myself?

'My mum *is* coming, just you wait and see,' I said.

'I'll be waiting – and we'll all be seeing,' said Justine About-To-Get-Her-Nose-Punched-Again Littlewood. 'We'll see my dad sitting there clapping away, but whoops, there'll be this *empty* seat right in the middle of the row where Mother Beaker's bottom should be, only she can't be bothered to come and see her only daughter – and who can blame her when she's as bonkers and batty and totally bananas as Tracy Beaker—'

I leaped up but Jenny caught hold of me and Mike hustled Justine out of the room.

'Cool it, Tracy,' said Jenny.

I couldn't cool it. I was burning up, about to erupt like a volcano. But then Peter clutched my hand.

'Take no notice of Justine. She's just jealous because you're such a brilliant actress and everyone signed my petition because they all know the play wouldn't work without you. And if you say your mum's coming, then of course she will. You always know everything, Tracy.'

I took a deep deep deep breath and then squeezed his hand.

'That's right, Peter,' I said. 'Thanks, pal. Don't fret. I wouldn't let a sad twisted girl like Justine wind me up.'

Jenny gave me a quick hug. 'Well done, girl.'

'Jenny?' I took another even deeper deeper deeper breath. 'I *know* my mum's coming, and I sent her all the details and all this stuff, but I don't suppose she's been on the phone just to *confirm* she's coming?'

'You know I'd have told you, Tracy.'

'Yeah, yeah, well . . . As if she *needs* to tell us. I mean, we can just take it as read, can't we?' I said.

'I'm coming,' said Jenny. 'And Mike. We're getting extra help here just so we can watch you. Elaine's coming. Don't pull that face, Tracy! Cam's coming. It will be wonderful if your mum comes too, but you'll still have lots of people in the audience absolutely rooting for you. OK?'

It wasn't OK at all. This was Careworker

Evasive-Speak. I *couldn't* take it as read that my mum was coming.

I knew that.

I didn't *want* to know.

I tried very very very hard indeed to take it as read. It was as if it was printed everywhere and I was literally reading it over and over again. I stared round the kitchen and saw it spelled out in spaghetti shapes all round the walls.

YOUR MUM'S COMING TO SEE YOU ACT SCROOGE

I went to the toilet and I saw it scribbled all over the door.

Your Mum's coming to see you act Scrooge.

I went to school in the minivan and I saw it flash up on the dashboard.

YOUR MUM'S COMING TO SEE YOU ACT SCROOGE

I looked out of the window and saw it on all the posters in town.

YOUR MUM'S COMING TO SEE YOU ACT SCROOGE

I got to school and it was chalked on the
blackboard.

Your Mum's coming to see you act Scrooge.

I stood in assembly and it shone above
the stage.

YOUR MUM'S COMING TO SEE YOU ACT SCROOGE.

The words flashed on and off in my mind all
day long like little fairy lights.

YOUR MUM'S COMING TO SEE YOU ACT SCROOGE.

I couldn't concentrate on a thing in class.
I thought Henry the Sixth had eight wives, I
couldn't even do short division, let alone long,
I ran the wrong way in the obstacle race in PE,
I coloured Santa's beard scarlet on my Christmas
card. Luckily Miss Brown just laughed at me.

'I know you've got other things on your mind
today, Tracy. Good luck with the play tonight. I'm
so looking forward to it.'

But I *didn't* have the play on my mind. I
couldn't get it *in* my mind. We had a last rehearsal

at lunch time, gabbling through our lines one last time. I stumbled and stuttered and couldn't remember a thing.

'I don't know what's gone wrong, Miss Simpkins!' I said frantically. 'I'm word perfect, I know I am. I could chant the whole play backwards yesterday, I swear I could.'

'I knew Tracy Beaker would mess up royally,' Justine whispered to Louise, though it was a loud enough whisper for me to hear.

'It's simply last-minute nerves, Tracy,' said Miss Simpkins. 'You'll be fine tonight. Don't worry about it.'

She was doing her best to be reassuring – but *she* looked worried. I could see her thinking, *Oh my Lord, I've gone out on a limb to keep problem kid Tracy in the play and now she can't even say a simple line! What have I done? I must keep smiling, stay calm. I'm not going to panic. I'll just tell the kid she'll be fine tonight.*

For the first and only time in my life I was in

total agreement with Justine Smug-Slug Littlewood. It looked like I was going to mess up royally.

We didn't go home for our tea. All the children in the cast had a packed picnic on my wondrously polished hall floor. If I'd been my usual self I'd have been incensed. They were spilling sandwich crumbs and scattering crisps all over the place. One of the kids even poured a carton of sticky squash all over my floor! But I was in such a state I barely noticed. I couldn't even eat my picnic. My egg sandwich tasted of old damp flannel, my crisps stuck in my throat, my yoghurt smelled sour.

'Eat up, Tracy. You're going to be burning up a lot of energy tonight,' said Peter. 'Here, do you want half my special banana sandwich? Hey, you can have all of it if you like.'

'Thanks, Pete – but no thanks,' I said.

I sat and brooded, snapping all my crisps into tiny golden splinters. I didn't know what to do.

I so so so wanted my mum to come and see me, but did I really want her to see me standing sweating on stage, mouth open, but no words whatsoever coming out?

I shut my eyes tight. 'Please, if there really is a Spirit of Christmas Past, a Spirit of Christmas Present and a Spirit of Christmas Yet to Come, help me now, and then I'll out-do Tiny Tim with my "God bless you"s,' I said inside my head.

 I sensed someone standing beside me. I opened my eyes, hoping desperately that it might be Mum, with her lovely long golden curls, her big blue eyes, her glossy pink lips all ready to kiss me . . . but I was staring at this small scruffy woman with short sticking-up hair.

'Oh, it's only you, Cam,' I said wearily.

'Happy Christmas to you too, Tracy,' said Cam, laughing.

'What are you doing here? The play's not for hours yet.'

'I know. I've come to help your Miss Simpkins do your make-up.'

'But you don't know anything about it! You never *wear* make-up.'

'I'm great at stage make-up, you wait and see.'

She sat down cross-legged beside me. She was wearing her usual jeans and jersey – but they were her newest not-frayed-at-the-hems jeans and she was wearing her best jumper with the knitted cats.

She thrust a big box of chocolates at me.

'Here. Have a nibble, then pass them round to all your pals.'

'Oh, Cam. Did you buy them specially for me?'

'Well, not exactly,' said Cam. 'They were going to be for my mum, when I went home for Christmas. Only I'm not actually *going* home as it turns out, so I thought we could have them now.'

'Well, it's very kind of you but I'm not a bit hungry. I feel kind of sick. Maybe I'm going to throw up on stage. If I do I hope it's when Justine's doing her Marley's Ghost bit,' I said.

I opened the box of chocolates all the same, simply out of curiosity. They were extra-special wonderful chocs, all sleek and shiny, some wrapped in pink and silver and gold paper, others dotted with cherries and nuts and little crystallized roses.

'Oh, yum,' I said automatically. My fingers reached out for the biggest cherry chocolate of their own accord. I gave it one little lick and then popped it in my mouth quick.

I chewed, and the most beautiful cherry chocolate taste oozed all over my tongue and round my teeth.

'Mmm!' I said. My hand reached out again.

'I wouldn't have too many if you're feeling sick,' said Cam.

'Do you know something weird? I'm starting to feel just a tiny bit better. Hey, these are seriously scrumptious chocolates. Do I really have to hand them round? I'll have just *one* more, OK? Your mum's really missing out big-time. Why aren't you going to see her at Christmas then?'

'Oh. We had a row. We always have rows. I phoned her to ask if I could bring someone with me.'

'Who? Not a boyfriend!'

'I've *told* you, Tracy, I haven't got a boyfriend. This was someone else, but anyway, she didn't like that idea, and then she went on about this party she's giving, and saying stuff like will I please have my hair done and could I wear a decent skirt and proper heels.' Cam sighed. 'She's impossible.'

'No, she's not. You'd look *heaps* better with your hair done all fancy and a nice tight skirt, and why on earth *don't* you wear heels? My mum always does.'

I shouldn't have said the word *mum*. My tummy went tight all over again. I was on my fourth chocolate by this time. It didn't seem such a great idea.

Cam held my hand. 'Your mum's obviously a glamorous girly mum. I'm more your *casual* woman. Though *my* mum would say there's casual and there's downright ragbag.'

'Oh, Cam, do *you* think my mum will come to see me act Scrooge?'

Cam gripped my hand tightly. 'I'm sure she *wants* to come, badly. It's just . . . she could be tied up somewhere.'

'I'm going to let her down if she *does* come.' I crept closer to Cam. I hissed in her ear so none of the other kids could hear. 'I was totally rubbish at the rehearsal at lunch time. I couldn't remember a single word.'

'That's great, Tracy,' said Cam brightly.

'That's *great*?' I said. 'Oh thanks, Cam! I thought you were supposed to be my *friend*? It's great that Tracy Beaker is going to publicly humiliate herself in front of the whole school, all the parents, everyone from the Dumping Ground and her own *mother*?'

'I *am* your friend and I'm talking sense. Everyone knows that it's bad luck to have a dress rehearsal that goes really well. The worse it is, the better the actual performance.'

'You're kidding!'

'No, no, it's common knowledge in the acting profession. I'm surprised your mum hasn't told you. So you'll be great tonight, Tracy, you'll see.'

'But I can't remember a single line! What am I meant to do? *Mime* it all?'

'Well, I'm sure you'd mime very expressively, but I don't think that will be necessary. The moment you get on stage I'm sure you'll be word perfect again. The lines are all in there, Tracy.'

She swung our clasped hands upwards and gently tapped my head. 'You just need to press the right button and they'll come bursting out as easily as anything, believe me.'

I looked at her. I *didn't* believe her – but I was touched that she was trying so hard to convince me. I looked at Cam's best outfit. I looked at her earnest face and her funny scrubbing-brush haircut. I suddenly gave her a big hug right there in front of everyone.

Some skinny little kid playing Ignorance in the play piped up, 'Is that your mum, Tracy?'

'She's not my *real* mum,' I said. 'But she's kind of *like* a mum to me.'

Cam gave me a big hug back. 'That's the nicest thing you've ever said about me, Tracy,' she said.

'It's all this Christmas Peace and Goodwill stuff. It's getting to me,' I said.

I passed all the chocolates round. I *even* offered one to Justine, which was a waste of time.

'You've probably gobbed all over them, Tracy Beaker,' she said.

Mrs Darlow came trit-trotting out of her office,

in through the swing doors and over my beautifully shiny floor to wish us all luck.

Miss Simpkins came scurrying to my side, looking tense. I smiled at her reassuringly and offered Mrs Darlow a chocolate.

'Good luck, Tracy Beaker,' she said, popping a nut cluster in her mouth.

'Mind how you go in those little heels, Mrs Darlow. We don't want you slipping on the highly polished floor,' I said politely.

'Ah, yes. You've worked hard, Tracy. It's a little patchy here and there, but on the whole you've done a splendid job. Nothing beats a bit of elbow grease. I'm almost tempted to do away with the electric polisher and employ you on a permanent basis.'

'You have an electric polisher?' I said faintly. 'Yet you let me polish the entire floor by *hand*?'

'Tracy!' Cam hissed.

I took a deep breath. 'So the hall floor *could* have been polished in a matter of minutes, Mrs Darlow?'

'But that wouldn't have been such an excellent . . . what was the phrase? A channel for your aggression!' said Mrs Darlow, smiling at me. Triumphantly.

I looked at her. She looked at me. Cam was on one side of me, Miss Simpkins on the other. I knew both were holding their breath.

I suddenly burst out laughing. 'Nice one, Mrs Darlow,' I said. 'You win.'

'Thank you,' said Mrs Darlow. 'So you win tonight, Tracy Beaker. Act your little socks off.'

She zigzagged her way through the picnicking cast as if she was performing a complicated country dance and went out of the hall.

Cam and Miss Simpkins blew out their cheeks and sighed 'Pheeeeeew' simultaneously.

'You both thought I was going to blow it, didn't you?' I said.

'Well, the thought did just cross my mind,' said Miss Simpkins.

'It crossed and recrossed and danced up and down in *my* mind,' said Cam. She scrabbled in the chocolate box, found another great big cherry

cream and popped it in my mouth. 'Here, kiddo, you deserve it.'

'Now, I suppose we'd better start getting the show on the road,' said Miss Simpkins. 'OK, kids, clear up your picnic stuff as quick as you can. I want all the stagehands to go up on the stage and start sorting out the backdrops. I'll come and help in a minute. All the rest of you, come and find your costumes. Then, once you're dressed, go to Cam to get made up.'

'I wish we had *proper* costumes,' Justine complained.

'I do too, Justine, but we haven't had the time, money or indeed expertise to assemble proper Victorian costumes for a large cast. We've done our best with limited resources,' Miss Simpkins said crisply.

We all had to wear our ordinary school uniform, with coats on for everyone playing men. We had cardboard top hats and cardboard bonnets tied with ribbon. The children carol singers simply wound woolly scarves around their necks.

Carol Singer

Victorian Gentleman

Victorian Lady

Marley's Ghost

Miss Simpkins did her best to be inventive with the ghost costumes. Justine as Marley's Ghost had a big bandage round her head and a long dog chain with keys and purses and cash-boxes attached to it with Scoubidou strings.

As the Spirit of Christmas Past, Louise had a white frock and a white veil and her hair brushed out loose past her

Spirit of Christmas Past

shoulders. She danced round and round, pointing her toes.

'I'm glad I've got a pretty costume,' she said.

The Spirit of Christmas Present wore a Santa hat with a white cotton-wool beard and he had sprigs of holly pinned all over him. You couldn't get too near or he'd prick you.

The Spirit of Christmas Yet to Come wore a long black velvet gown (actually Miss Simpkins's dressing gown!) with a black scarf over his head.

Spirit of Christmas Present

Spirit of Christmas Yet to Come

Tiny Tim

That just left Peter and me. He didn't have a special costume as Tiny Tim, just a little cap and a crutch made out of an old broom handle.

I had *two* costumes. I wore my school shirt and grey trousers and an old grey raincoat cut at the back to make proper tails. I also had a white nightshirt with a white cap and slippers with pompoms for my night-time scenes.

Everyone laughed when I tried on the nightshirt, and started spreading rumours that it was *Mrs Darlow's* nightie. I started capering around doing a rude imitation of Mrs Darlow, sticking my bum right out and waggling it. Everyone laughed and I laughed too – though inside I felt so wound up I felt more like crying.

Was my mum going to come???

And if she did, would I let her down?

My capers got wilder. Cam collared me by the scruff of the nightshirt.

'Hey, hey, how about saving the acting for when you go on stage? Get into your Scrooge day outfit and then come to Classroom One. I'll do your make-up first, OK?'

'I don't want any experimenting! You're a total novice when it comes to make-up, Cam.'

'I tell you, I'm a dab hand at stage make-up, trust me. Come on, kiddo. You need to simmer down a little. There's no point being diplomatic with Mrs Darlow one minute and then sending her up rotten the next. If she walked in on your impersonation you'd be toast, Ms Beaker.'

We went to Classroom One together and she got out this huge case of make-up. She plonked me down on a chair and put a towel round my shoulders. She brushed my hair and yanked it into a tight topknot and then crammed a weird wig on my head, half pink rubber for a big bald patch, with straggly grey bits trailing to my shoulders.

'Now for your Scrooge face,' she said, starting to rub pale panstick into my skin.

'Hey, careful! You're getting it in my eyes!'

'Well close them, silly. Come on, Tracy, you want to look the part, don't you? Stop squirming round and act sensible.'

I sat still as a statue, eyes closed, while Cam dabbed and smeared at my face and then stuck stuff all over my eyebrows. She breathed heavily with concentration, tutting if I so much as twitched. Then she patted me lightly under the chin.

'There, Scrooge! You're done.'

I opened my eyes. Cam was holding a mirror in front of me. A mean whey-faced old man with whiskery eyebrows and grey frown lines peered back at me. I gasped – and the old man's thin lips gasped too.

It was me! I could hardly believe it I looked so different.

'I don't look like me any more!'

'Of course you don't. You're *not* you. You're Ebenezer Scrooge, the meanest man in the city.'

'I look *exactly* like the picture in the book I sent my mum . . .' My voice tailed away.

Cam put her face close to mine, her brown eyes big and pleading.

'Tracy. Listen to me. You know sometimes your mum hasn't been able to come to see you because she's making a movie somewhere? Well, that's because she knows how important it is to concentrate on her part. That's what you've got to do now. You're not Tracy Beaker any more, desperate to see her mum. You're Scrooge, and you haven't *got* a mum or a dad or anyone at all. You're a mean old misery-guts who hates everyone, and you especially hate this time of year, Christmas, the season of goodwill, because you don't wish anyone well and you think Christmas is total humbug. Think yourself into the character, Tracy. Don't go and mess around with the others. Stay centred on what you're doing.'

'Bah!' I said. 'Out of my way, Missy. Let me get back to my counting house. I need to give that varmint clerk of mine, Bob Cratchit, a severe talking to.'

Cam grinned and bobbed her head at me. 'Beg pardon, I'm sure, Mr Scrooge,' she said.

So I sloped off into Classroom Two and paced up and down the room telling myself I was Scrooge Scrooge Scrooge. Peter popped his head round the door and asked if I was OK.

'Bah! Humbug!' I growled.

He jumped back, looking upset. 'Sorry, Tracy!'

'I'm not Tracy, I'm Scrooge, you ignorant little lad. When I've been visited by Old Marley and the three Christmas Ghosts I shall have a change of heart and look on you kindly, almost as my own son, but for the moment, hop it!'

Peter hopped it. Literally, using his crutch.

I was fine all the time I was by myself. I thought myself into being Scrooge and acted some of the scenes, bending over like a gnarled old man. But then Miss Simpkins came to find me.

'Ah, Tracy, Cam said you were in here. You make an utterly splendid Scrooge – quite scary! OK, sweetheart, fifteen minutes to go till curtain up. Better whizz to the toilet and then come backstage with all the others.'

Suddenly I got so so so scared I stopped being

Scrooge. I didn't even feel like Tracy Beaker any more. I felt like this tiny trembly mini-mouse. My voice turned into a squeak. I had to fight not to hang onto Miss Simpkins's hand like some silly little kid in the Infants. I wanted Cam but she was still making people up in Classroom One.

I had to go and join Justine Hate-Her-Guts Littlewood and Louise and Peter and all the others. They were supposed to be sitting cross-legged at the back of the stage, only speaking in whispers. Of course they were all over the place, giggling and gossiping, clowning around in their

costumes. The red velvet stage curtains were pulled shut but Justine ran up to them and had a little peep out.

'I can see him! There's my dad! My dad's right at the front! Hey, Dad, Dad, here I am!'

Then all the children rushed to the gap in the curtains, sticking their heads out and peering.

All the children except me.

I hung back. I thought of all those chairs, row after row to the back of the hall. I thought of my mum. I willed her to be sitting there right at the front, but *not* next to Justine's dad. I wanted her to be there so much it was as if I had laser eyes that could bore right through the thick crimson velvet. There she was, sitting on the edge of her seat, smiling, waving, her pink heart gleaming round her neck . . .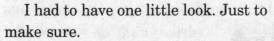

I had to have one little look. Just to make sure.

I elbowed Justine Big-Bottom Littlewood out of the way and put one eye to the gap between the curtains. The hall was absolutely heaving, with almost every seat taken. I saw all the parents and the wriggly little brothers and sisters. I saw Jenny and Mike. I saw Elaine. She'd taken off her antlers but she had a sprig of mistletoe tied rakishly over one ear (who would want to kiss *Elaine*?). I saw Cam shunting along the front row, finished with her make-up session, every last member of the cast pansticked into character. I saw Justine's awful dad with his gold medallion and his tight leather jacket. I saw everyone . . . except my mum.

I looked right along every single row. She wasn't there. She wasn't in the front. She wasn't in the middle. She wasn't at the back.

Maybe she'd got held up. She'd be jumping out of her stretch limo right this minute, running precariously in her high heels, teeter-tottering up the school drive and now here she was . . .

Not yet.

Any second now.

I stared and stared and stared.

Then I felt a hand on my shoulder.

'Get into place on stage, Tracy. We're about to start,' Miss Simpkins said softly.

'But my mum hasn't come yet! Can't we wait five minutes more? I don't want her to miss the beginning.'

'We'll wait one minute then. You go and settle yourself in your counting-house chair. I'll go and get the carol singers assembled. Then we'll *have* to start, sweetheart.'

'I can't. Not without my mum.'

'You're going to have to, Tracy. The show must

go on,' said Miss Simpkins.

I didn't care about the show now. There wasn't any point acting Scrooge if my mum couldn't see me. I clutched my chest. It really hurt. Maybe it was my heart breaking.

'I couldn't act to save my life,' I said.

'What about acting to save *my* life?' said Miss Simpkins. 'And what about Cam? What about little Peter and all the children who signed his petition? You can't let them down, Tracy.'

I knew she was right. I swallowed very very very hard to get rid of the lump in my throat. I blinked very very very hard to get rid of the water in my eyes. I took a deep deep deep breath.

'Bah!' I said. 'Humbug!'

Miss Simpkins gave me a thumbs-up and then beetled off to cue the carol singers. I sat in my chair, hunched up. They started singing 'Once in Royal David's City'. I started singing my own mournful little version:

'Once in poxy London city
Stood a lowly primary school
Where this girl waits for her mother
To come and see her act the fool.
Carly is that mother wild
Tracy Beaker is that child.'

Then the curtains parted with a swish, the lights went on dimly to show my candle-lit counting house, and I sat tensely in my chair, scowling.

I hated the noise of the chirpy carol singers. All *their* mums and dads were watching them, oohing and aahing and whispering, 'Ah, *bless*.'

My mum wasn't there. She couldn't be bothered to come, even though I'd bought her all those presents. She didn't care tuppence about me.

Well, I didn't care tuppence about her. I didn't care tuppence about *anyone*. I stomped to the side of the stage and shook my fist at the carol singers as they all cried, 'Happy Christmas!'

'Bah!' I said. 'Humbug. Be off with you!'

I felt as if I'd truly turned into Scrooge. My nephew came to wish me Merry Christmas and I sent him off with a flea in his ear. I didn't want to make merry with him. I bullied my stupid clerk Bob Cratchit, and then had a bite to eat. I ate my chicken drumstick like a finicky old man, and when one of the little kids played being a dog on all fours I snatched the bone away and shook my fist at him. He growled at me and I growled back. I heard the audience laugh. Someone whispered, 'Isn't that Tracy Beaker a proper caution!'

Then I went to bed and Justine Enemy-For-Ever Littlewood clanked on stage as Marley's Ghost, the coffin bandage round her head, her long chain trailing keys and padlocks and coinboxes.

Justine's ridiculous dad started clapping wildly before she'd so much as opened her mouth and Justine Utterly-Unprofessional Littlewood totally forgot she was Marley's Ghost. She turned and waved excitedly at her father, just like a five-year-old in her first Nativity play.

I gave a gasp to remind Justine she was there to spook me out and give me a warning. Justine shuffled towards me unwillingly, still peering round at her dad. Her chain tangled around her feet. She wasn't looking where she was going. Recipe for disaster!

Justine tripped over her own padlock and went flying, landing flat on her face.

She lay there, looking a total idiot. Her face was all screwed up. She was trying not to cry.

My chest hurt. I knew just how she felt, falling over and making such a fool of herself in front of her dad. I reached out a shaking hand.

'Is it you, Jacob Marley, my old partner? It *can't* be you, because you're as dead as a doornail.' That was in Miss Simpkins's script. Now it was time for a spot of improvisation. 'Yet it must be you, Marley. You were unsteady on your feet in your last few years on earth – and you're unsteady now in your present spirit situation. Allow me to assist you, old chap.'

I took hold of Justine and hauled her up. The audience clapped delightedly because I'd saved the situation.

'Pray tell me why you're fettered,' I said, following the script again.

'I wear the chain I forged in life,' said Justine, pulling herself together. She sounded pretty miserable, but that was in character.

Then I was visited by Louise as the Spirit of Christmas Past. She'd put her own make-up on over Cam's so she looked more like she was going out clubbing than off haunting mean old men, but at least she didn't fall over.

We acted out the bit where little boy Scrooge was sent to a horrible boarding school and told he couldn't ever go home. It was a bit like me being sent off to the Dumping Ground.

I thought about Mum sending me there and not coming back to fetch me. Not even coming today, when I was starring as Scrooge. Tears rolled down my cheeks. I don't ever cry. But I wasn't being Tracy Beaker; I was acting Scrooge, and doing it so well I heard several snuffles in the audience. They were moved to tears too by my brilliant performance!

I had a chance to blow my nose on my nightshirt hem while everyone danced at the Fezziwigs' party. Then the curtains closed and the carol singers stood in front and sang 'Away in a Manger'.

I sang my own version to myself:

> 'Away in a schoolhouse
> No mum watched her daughter
> But Little Tracy Beaker
> Acted incredibly – she didn't falter!'

Miss Simpkins and a host of little helpers rushed round the stage scattering real holly and ivy and mistletoe and fake painted plaster turkeys, ham, mince pies and clementines.

Then the curtains opened and I peered out, waving the carol singers away and going 'Ssh! Ssh!' to the audience. Fat Freddy waddled on stage in his Father Christmas outfit as the Spirit of Christmas Present and took me to see the Cratchit family.

Peter was shaking all over, scared out of his wits, but the moment he hopped across the stage using his crutch everyone went 'Aaah! Doesn't he look *sweet*!' When he said, 'God bless us every one,' they all started clapping.

It looked as if weedy little Peter had stolen the show.

It was *my* show. I was Scrooge. I wanted them just to clap *me*. But Peter was my friend. He'd tried so hard for me. My chest hurt again. He liked me so much. And I liked him. I really did. Maybe I was a little bit glad he was being such a success. When the Spirit of Christmas Present told me Tiny Tim was going to die I cried straight from the heart, 'No, no! Oh no, kind Spirit! Say he will be spared!'

Then, as midnight struck, I spotted the two tiny children hiding under the Spirit's robes, the smallest skinniest kids Miss Simpkins could find, one playing Ignorance and one playing Want.

The last Spirit came creeping onto the stage,

draped in a long black robe, the scary Spirit of Christmas Yet to Come. The lights were very low so it looked as if we were wandering through the night together. We went to the Cratchit house, so melancholy without Tiny Tim. Then we went to the graveyard. Miss Simpkins shone a torch on the great cardboard tombstone. I saw my own name written there, Ebenezer Scrooge. I trembled and threw myself down on my knees.

'Oh, Spirit, have mercy!' I cried. 'Tell me I can sponge away the writing on this stone. I have learned my lesson. I will honour Christmas in my heart and try to keep it all the year.'

HERE LIES EBENEZER SCROOGE

Then the lights went out and I jumped into my own bed quick as a wink and then acted waking up on Christmas Day. The carol singers sang 'We Wish You a Merry Christmas' outside my window. I sprang out of bed, did a little caper in my nightgown, and then went and called out to them.

'I wish you a Merry Christmas too, dear fellows. A Merry Christmas and a Happy New Year, and I, Ebenezer Scrooge, am going to lead a happy new life.'

Bells rang out and I danced up and down. Then I put my coat on over my nightshirt and rushed off stage, staggering back with the most comically enormous turkey, almost as big as me. I invited everyone to my house for Christmas. The whole cast crammed on stage and we 'ate' plastic mince pies and quaffed pretend wine – even Marley's Ghost and the three Christmas Spirits – and then we all sang 'God Rest Ye Merry Gentlemen'.

God rest ye merry gentlemen, let nothing you dismay...

I got Peter to shout out, 'God bless us every one!' right at the end.

Then the clapping started. It went on and on and on. We all stood holding hands and bowing. The four Ghosts got a special bow. Then Peter had to bow all by himself. He was so excited he did a little hoppy dance, waving his crutch, and the audience roared.

Then it was my turn. I stood in front of all the others. Cam and Jenny and Mike and Elaine stood up and started clapping and clapping. Miss Simpkins at the side of the stage was clapping and clapping. *Mrs Darlow* at the back of the hall was clapping and clapping. All the mums and dads were clapping and clapping.

But my mum wasn't clapping. She wasn't there.

HURRAH! Clap Clap Clap
BRAVO!
Clap Clap Clap
Clap
MORE!
Clap
Clap
Clap
Clap
Clap
BRAVO!
Clap
Clap Clap Clap
Clap
MORE!
Clap
Clap Clap

It was the proudest moment of my life. I'd acted Scrooge and I'd been *good* at it. Glorious. Magnificent. The audience shouted '*Bravo!*' And '*Good for Tracy!*' And '*What a little star!*'

Mum didn't know. Mum didn't care.

I had a smile all over my face and yet my eyes were going blink blink blink. I was in serious danger of having an attack of hay fever in front of everyone.

Miss Simpkins came out onto the stage holding an enormous bunch of red roses and white lilies done up with a huge red satin ribbon.

'They've just arrived, Tracy. They're for you,' she said, handing them over.

There was a card inside.

Congratulations, my little star.
Wish I could have seen you.
Lots of love, mum xxx

'It's from my *mum*!' I said – but the note proved *fatal* for my hay fever. Still, everyone knows flowers trigger hay-fever attacks. I wasn't crying. I don't *ever* cry.

Then we had a proper party in the hall with real mince pies for everyone. Cam came and hugged me hard and said she was so very proud of me.

'You were totally brilliant, Tracy,' she said. 'And there's you saying you couldn't remember a word!'

'Well, it didn't *feel* as if I was remembering it.

It wasn't like *acting*. It was as if I was really living it,' I said.

'Aha! That shows you're a *real* actor,' said Cam.

'Like Mum,' I said.

'Just like your mum.' Cam smiled at me. 'Aren't they gorgeous flowers? Wasn't it lovely of her to send them? Imagine, getting your own huge bouquet of flowers.'

'Yeah. With a lovely note. Did you see what my mum wrote?'

'Yes, Tracy.'

'The only thing is . . .' I swallowed. 'It's not my mum's handwriting.'

I looked hard at Cam. She didn't look away. She stared straight into my eyes.

'Of course it's not your mum's actual writing, Tracy. You order the flowers on the phone and say what you want on the card and then the local florist writes it down.'

'Oh!' I said. I swallowed again. The mince pie seemed made of very lumpy pastry. 'You wouldn't kid me, would you, Cam?'

'No one could ever kid you, Tracy Beaker,' said Cam.

'Well, I think it was lovely of my mum. But it would have been a lot lovelier if she'd actually come to see me,' I said.

'I'm sure she would have done if she possibly could,' said Cam.

'Do you think she's still coming to see me on Christmas Day?' I said.

'Well . . . maybe she is,' said Cam.

'And maybe she's not,' I said. 'So what am I going to do on Christmas Day, eh? I *hate* Christmas in the Dumping Ground. Jenny and Mike try hard but they've always got the little kids clinging to them and everyone tears open their presents too quickly and then fusses because they think the others have got better things, and there's never enough new batteries and often the stuff doesn't work anyway. We watch television but all the programmes are about families and we are all so *not* a family. We have turkey and Christmas pudding for dinner because Jenny wants it to be traditional so we don't miss out, but I don't really *like* turkey or Christmas pudding – though I eat too much anyway – and then we're supposed to play these crazy games but the little kids are too dim to play and the big kids just want to slope off to their rooms and someone always throws a tantrum because they're so fed up and lonely and left out. That someone is quite often me, as a matter of fact.'

'Hmm,' said Cam. 'It sounds as if we both have crap Christmases. Tell you what, Tracy. Let's join up together. You come to me for Christmas. What do you think?'

'I think that sounds a brilliant idea,' I said.

So that's exactly what I did. I woke up very early on Christmas morning and opened all my presents peacefully, all by myself. Jenny gave me cool new jeans and a CD and Mike gave me new trainers and amazing black nail varnish. Elaine gave me a *little fluffy blue teddy bear* – yuck yuck yuck! Peter gave me a silver yo-yo. It was very sweet of him. I decided to give him the blue teddy.

My mum didn't give me anything.

I expect the roses and lilies cost a lot of money. Acting is a chancy profession. Maybe Mum was a bit strapped for cash at the moment.

Of course, Grizelda Moonbeam might work her magic and Mum might appear in person, weighed down with presents. But somehow it wasn't starting to seem very likely. It didn't look as if I was going to be spending this festive occasion with my Loved One. Unless . . . maybe *Cam* counted as a Loved One? Was I *her* Loved One?? Had the charm actually worked a double whammy???

I knew Cam was certainly short of money so I wasn't too hopeful about her present to me. She arrived astonishingly early. She was wearing a woolly hat and scarf and mittens, with a big woolly jumper over her jeans and woolly socks.

'Happy Christmas, Cam! Have you got woolly *knickers* on? Why are you all bundled up? And you're so *early*. We haven't even had breakfast yet. Do you want some?'

'Happy Christmas, Tracy. You need to pile on lots of woolly jumpers too. We're going for a walk. And we're having breakfast out, OK?'

She drove us for miles to this big park. It wasn't snowing but it was still early enough for there to be a frost so we could kid ourselves it was a real white Christmas.

'Come on!' said Cam, parking the car. She opened the door. It certainly *felt* frosty. I hadn't got quite enough woollies.

'It's freezing, Cam! Can't we stay in the car?'

'We're going for a walk, Tracy, to work up an appetite for our breakfast.'

'You go for a walk. I'll stay in the car and watch you,' I said.

She dragged me out, rammed her own woolly hat over my head, wound her scarf round and round and round me as if she was wrapping a mummy, and then took me by the hand.

'There! Cosy now? Off we go!'

'I'm not really *into* long country walks, Cam. I'm not built for it. Look at my spindly legs.' I made my knees knock together and walked with a Tiny Tim limp.

'Just come down this path with me,' said Cam, tugging me. 'Through the trees. You'll like what you see when you get to the end.'

I knew what I'd see. *Scenery*. A lot more trees and a hill or two. I didn't see the point. Still, it was Christmas after all. I didn't want to be too difficult. I sighed and staggered after Cam. I didn't get why she wanted to stay out in the cold, especially before breakfast.

'I don't want to moan, but my tummy's rumbling rather a lot. It's saying, *Tracy, Tracy, what's happened to my cornflakes?*'

'You'll have breakfast very soon, I promise,' said Cam, laughing.

'Are we having a picnic then?' I asked.

It seemed a mad time of year to have a picnic and I didn't see any signs of a hamper. Cam wasn't carrying so much as a lunch box. Perhaps she had a sandwich or two crammed in her pockets? It looked like it was going to be a very *little* picnic, yet I was totally *starving*.

Cam and I weren't the only ones embarking

on this mad early-morning Starve-In. There were lots of other cars in the car park and little bunches of bobble-hatted muffled weirdos trudged along too, all heading in the same direction. It was like we were all in *Doctor Who* and some alien force was messing with our heads, controlling our minds.

Then we rounded a bend. I saw a big pond in the distance. A lot of people were *in* the pond. No, no, they were *on* it, gliding across.

'They're skating!' I said.

'Yep.'

'Can *we* skate?'

'We'll have a go.'

'But we haven't got any skates.'

'You can hire them, Tracy, I checked. And they're serving a special Christmas breakfast.'

'Oh, wow! So you planned it all? Oh, Cam, you have some seriously cool ideas.'

I gave her a quick hug and then started running helter-skelter to the ice. There was a big van serving golden croissants and hot chocolate with whipped cream. We had breakfast first, just to fortify ourselves, and then we hired our skates, held hands and hobbled onto the ice.

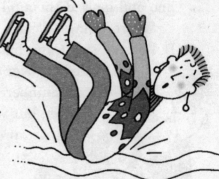

I thought I'd glide off like a swan, swoop-swoop, swirl-swirl, the epitome of athletic grace. Ha! I staggered like a drunk, clonk-clunk, whizz, whoops, bonk on my bum. Cam pulled me up, trying not to laugh.

'Look, Tracy, point your boots out and do it like *this*,' she said, demonstrating.

Some kid hurtled past her, making her jump. She wavered, wobbled – and then went bonk on *her* bum.

I *did* laugh and Cam laughed too.

'I don't know about woolly knickers. I think we both need *padded* knickers,' she said as I pulled her up.

We held onto each other and tried again. This time we staggered all the way round the pond. I started to get more daring. I tried a little swoop.

It worked! I tried another – left, right, truly gliding – only I couldn't seem to stop. I went charging straight into a little cluster of kids in a line and mowed them all down.

'We're going to have to rename you Tracy Bulldozer,' said Cam, hauling us all up.

We skated for over an hour, losing count of the number of times we both fell over, but we could also both glide properly for a few seconds at a time, so considered ourselves champion skaters.

'I think we deserve another breakfast after all that effort,' said Cam, and we polished off *another* croissant and mug of hot chocolate.

Then Cam drove us back to her house. She had a little Christmas tree in her living room.

'I usually don't bother, but they were selling them half price in the market yesterday so I decided to go mad.'

'It looks a bit naked if you don't mind me saying so. Aren't you meant to have little glass balls and tinsel and fairy lights?' I said.

'Of course you are. I thought it would be fun if we decorated the tree together,' said Cam. 'Look in that big carrier bag. There's all the decorations.'

'Oh, fantastic! We don't have a proper tree at the Dumping Ground because the little kids are so dopey they might mistake the glass balls for apples and the big kids are so rowdy they might knock it all over. I've *always* wanted to decorate a tree!'

'Then be my guest. I'll go and sort out what we might be having for Christmas dinner. I know you don't go a bundle on turkey and I'm mostly veggie nowadays . . . I could do a sort of tofu and vegetable casserole?'

'That sounds absolutely temptingly delicious – *not*!' I said.

'I rather thought that would be your response. I don't fancy faffing around in the kitchen for hours anyway. How about egg and chips?'

'Now you're talking! With lots of tomato sauce?'

'You can dollop it all over your plate, Tracy. It's Christmas. Ah! What else do you get at Christmas? We've got a Christmas tree. We'll have our Christmas dinner. But there's something else you have at Christmas. Um. What could it be? Oh yes! Presents!'

She opened up a cupboard and pulled out three parcels in jolly Santa wrapping paper tied with red ribbon.

'Oh, Cam! Are they for me?'

'Well, they've all got Tracy Beaker on the labels, so if that's your name I'd say it was a safe bet they're all for you.'

I felt really really really great. Cam had bought me loads of lovely presents.

I felt really really really bad. I hadn't got Cam anything.

'Oh dear, why the saddo face? Did you hope there might be more?' Cam teased.

'*You* haven't got any presents, Cam!' I wailed.

'Yes I have. I've opened mine already. I got a silk *headscarf* from my mum – as if I'd ever wear it! Plus a posh credit-card holder when I'm so overdrawn I can't use my blooming cards anyway. I got lovely presents from my friends though. Jane gave me my woolly hat and scarf and mittens and Liz gave me a big box of chocs and a book token.'

'What's a book *token*?'

'It's a little card for a certain amount of money and when you take it to a shop you can change it for any book you fancy.'

'Oh, I get it.' I nodded. 'Good idea!'

'Come on then, open your presents from me.'

I opened the heaviest first. It was ten children's paperbacks. They were all a bit dog-eared and tattered.

'I'm afraid they're second-hand,' said Cam. 'I searched in all the charity shops. A lot of them were ten-pence bargains!'

I eyed them suspiciously. 'They're classics,' I said. 'Aren't they, like, boring?'

'Is *A Christmas Carol* boring? No! These were all my favourites when I was your age. Cam Lawson's Top Ten Super Reads for kids your age. If you don't want them I'll have a great time re-reading them. *Little Women* is about this family of sisters and they like acting too, and reading Charles Dickens. You'll especially like Jo, who's a tomboy and wants to be a writer.

'Then there's *Black Beauty*. It's a wonderful story, and there's a very sad bit about a horse called Ginger which always makes me cry, but it's lovely all the same. *What Katy Did* is about a big family – Katy's the eldest, and she's always in heaps of trouble but then she falls off a swing and can't walk for ages. She's got a very saintly cousin who irritates a bit, but it's a great story, truly.

'*The Wind in the Willows* is about a mole

and a rat who are great chums and
they have this pal Toad who's a
terrible show-off, and there are some
very funny bits. *Five Children and It*
is also funny – it's about these kids who
meet a sand fairy and all their wishes come
true, but they always go wrong.'

'Chance would be a fine thing,' I said,
sniffing.

'There's also *Mary Poppins*. The book's
much better than the film. I loved *Tom
Sawyer* because he's very badly behaved
and always in trouble, and you might give
Anne of Green Gables a go. It's all about
this little orphan girl who won't ever
stop talking. You'll identify big-time
with those two.

'I'm sure you'll like *The Secret
Garden* because Mary is wondrously
grouchy and rude to everyone and has
to live in a house with a hundred rooms
on the Yorkshire Moors. And
Ballet Shoes is a perfect
book for you, because these
three sisters go to a stage
school and perform in lots

of plays, and I think that's maybe what you might end up doing, Tracy.'

'OK, OK. I'll give them a go,' I said. 'I can always share them with some of the other kids, eh? Peter might like the Mole and Rat and Toad book.'

I tried the next parcel, the biggest. It had a big drawing book, a big pail of felt tips and a giant tub of modelling clay, all different colours. These were all brand new!

'I thought it was about time you had your own art supplies instead of raiding poor Elaine's art cupboard,' said Cam.

'Oh wow! I'm *not* going to share these!'

Finally I picked up the tiniest parcel. I unwrapped it and found a little black box.

I opened it up – and there was a silver star pin badge.

'It's for you, Tracy Beaker Superstar,' said Cam, pinning it on me.

I gave her a big big big hug.

Then I decorated the tree, carefully dangling each glass ball and chocolate Santa and little bird and twirly glass icicle, while Cam wound the fairy lights round and round. When we switched them on the tree looked totally magical.

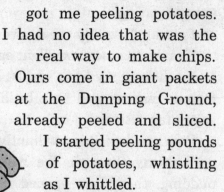

Then I helped Cam cook the lunch. She got me peeling potatoes. I had no idea that was the real way to make chips. Ours come in giant packets at the Dumping Ground, already peeled and sliced. I started peeling pounds of potatoes, whistling as I whittled.

'Steady on, girl. There's just the two of us,' said Cam.

'I never get quite *enough* chips at the Dumping Ground,' I said.

'OK. It's Christmas. Today you can eat until you burst,' said Cam.

She wouldn't let me fry them in the big

sizzling chip pan, but she *did* let me
fry our eggs and that was great fun.
We both had *enormous* piles
of golden chips on our
plates, with a fried egg
on top like snow on
a mountain peak.
I squirted mine
liberally with scarlet
sauce and then we
started eating. I ate
and ate and ate. My meal was delicious.

'I make the most excellent egg and chips ever,'
I said, licking my lips. 'Maybe I'm going to be a
famous chef as well as a brilliant writer and a
superstar actress.'

Cam ate her chips valiantly but had to give
up halfway through. We had clementines for
pudding, then Cam opened up her big box of
chocolates from Liz and we snaffled some of
those.

Then Cam undid her jeans and lay on the sofa,
groaning, while I got my new art stuff and started
creating. Cam rubbed her tummy, reached for a
book and started reading me the first Christmassy
chapter of *Little Women*. It was quite good in

an old-fashioned sort of way. Meg was a bit of a goody-goody and Beth was a bit wet and Amy was too pert and girly but I *loved* Jo.

Cam's voice tailed away after a while and she dozed off. I carried on and on and on creating. Then, when she started yawning and stretching and opening her eyes, I went and made her a cup of tea. No one has ever shown me how to do it but I'm not a total moron.

'Thank you, Tracy!' said Cam. She took a sip. 'Delicious!'

(I spotted her fishing several of the teabags out of her cup and spooning out a few of the still melting sugar lumps, but neither of us mentioned this.)

'I've got you some Christmas presents after all,' I said. 'Look on your coffee table.' I pointed proudly.

Cam nearly spilled her tea. 'Oh my lord! Multiple Tracy Beakers!' she said.

'Aren't they great!' I said. 'I made them with my modelling clay. The pink face was fine, and the red jumper and the blue skirt, but making my black curls all squiggly took *ages*.'

'Are all six for me?' said Cam.

'No, no. You have *this* one. She's the best, with the biggest smile. And I've got one for Peter and one for Jenny and one for Mike, and I suppose I ought to give one to Elaine and I thought I'd give one to Miss Simpkins when I go back to school.'

'That's a lovely idea. Well, I shall treasure my Tracy Beaker model. I'll put her on my desk. She can keep me company when I'm writing.'

'Don't crumple her up by mistake if you get stuck!' I said. 'Look, you've got another present.'

I handed her a folded piece of paper with a picture of me on the front.

'Oh, a card. How lovely!' said Cam.

'It's not a card. It's a Tracy token,' I said. 'You know, like a book token. But you don't get books with this token, you get *me*. Look inside.'

I'd written:

To Cam. Happy Christmas! 🌿🍒🌿

I, Tracy Beaker, promise to make you a plate of my famous egg and chips whenever I'm round at your place. 🍳 I will make you DOUBLE egg and chips on your birthday. 🍳

If I get to be a famous chef with my own swanky restaurant I will create a famous egg and chips dish and call it my <u>Cam Christmas Special.</u>

If I get to be a famous writer I will dedicate my second book to you. I hope that's okay, but I have to dedicate my first book to my mum.  📓 Tracy Beaker's 2nd Novel!

If I get to be a famous superstar actress I will let you be my drama coach. 😄😢

And if you finish your classes and go through with fostering me I will be the best foster daughter ever.

Love from
Tracy
XXX

Cam read it through, sniffling. 'Oh, Tracy,' she said. 'This is the best Christmas present I've ever had. And of course you'll be the best foster daughter ever. You're *Tracy Beaker*.'

Yes I am. Tracy Beaker Superstar.

When I went to bed that night back at the Dumping Ground I gave Mum's photo a kiss.

'I hope you had a Happy Christmas, Mum,' I whispered. 'Maybe see you next year, yeah?'

Then I lay back in bed and sang a little Christmas carol to myself.

'*Silent night, holy night,*
Tracy is calm, Tracy is bright.
Mum didn't come but I had a good time,
I love Mum but I'm glad Cam is mine.
Now I'll sleep in heavenly peace,
S-l-e-e-p in heav-en-ly peeeace.'

✳ • ✳ • ✳ • ✳ • ✳ • ✳ • ✳ • ✳ • ✳

✳ PRESENT WRAPPING TIPS ✳

- When you're choosing your wrapping paper, why not pick a different colour for each friend or family member, so their gifts are personalised? Or, if you're going to use the same wrapping paper for each person, try a different coloured ribbon for them all.

- If you don't like brightly coloured or glittery paper, plain brown paper and white string looks really elegant – and you can add a touch of colour with a holly leaf stuck on top.

- If you don't have any wrapping paper at all, see if you have any plain white drawing paper, and design your own Christmas pattern with coloured pencils, felt tips, glitter, and anything else you can find. Red and green are the most Christmassy colours, but you could try a multi-coloured rainbow theme too!

- Try personalising your gift tags for each person with a joke or poem. You could even write a line from a song that makes you think of that person. Or you could decorate the tag with pictures of things that remind you of them, like their favourite foods, or symbols to represent their hobbies.

✳ • ✳ • ✳ • ✳ • ✳ • ✳ • ✳ • ✳ • ✳

- Before you get started, make sure you have scissors and enough sticky tape for all the presents you're going to wrap – you don't want to run out halfway through! Cut off your bits of sticky tape and rest them loosely on the edge of the roll of tape, so you can grab them easily when you need them.

- Roll your wrapping paper out flat. Lay each present on it to check how much paper you need to cover it, before you start to cut. Remember the ends of the paper should overlap by a couple of centimetres, so that none of your present is left uncovered or sticking out!

- If you have several presents of different sizes for one person, try stacking them in a pile, biggest at the bottom and smallest at the top, in a sort of pyramid shape. Then use a long, wide ribbon to tie them all together, and tie a big bow at the top.

- If you have any wrapping paper left over, don't throw it away, even if you only have a few small scraps! Rip it up into tiny pieces and use it to stuff gift boxes or gift bags.

❋ PRESENTS AND PUZZLES ❋

How much do you know about Christmas? Take this
festive quiz to find out, and test your friends too.
You'll find the answers on page 248.

1. It's traditional to exchange a Christmas kiss
   under which plant?

2. In the poem 'The Night Before Christmas', what
   sweet treats are the children dreaming of?

3. What item of a traditional Christmas dinner
   is set alight before being eaten?

4. Which saint is now known as Santa Claus
   or Father Christmas?

5. Who makes a special speech every Christmas,
   which was first broadcast over the radio,
   and is now shown on television too?

6. What must happen for it to be a 'white
   Christmas'?

* · * · * · * · * · * · * · * · *

7. Mince pies are now filled with fruit, but what did they used to contain?

8. Which of these is not one of Santa's reindeer: Comet, Prancer, Klaxon, Blitzen?

9. What item is hidden inside a Christmas pudding and is said to bring good luck to whoever finds it in their piece?

10. In *The Little Match Girl*, the main character has a vision of a beautiful Christmas tree. Which author wrote this story?

11. Charles Dickens wrote the famous novel *A Christmas Carol*. What is the name of the main character in that book?

12. How many sides does a snowflake have?

13. On the second day of Christmas, what did my true love give to me?

14. People usually place one of two things at the top of their Christmas tree. One is an angel; what is the other?

15. What date is it traditional to take your Christmas tree down, otherwise known as Twelfth Night?

16. In the seventeenth century, who banned Christmas in England for several years?

* · * · * · * · * · * · * · * · *

17. The tallest snowman in the world was built in which country?

18. What two plants are often used as decorations at Christmas, are the title of a famous Christmas carol, and are also girls' names?

19. Name the three Wise Men.

20. Which famous novel starts with the line, 'Christmas won't be Christmas without any presents'?
(Here's a clue – it's one of Jacqueline's favourites!)

How many words can you make out of these letters in three minutes? Find a piece of paper to write them down. Time yourself and then challenge your friends!

DINGDONGMERRILYONHIGH

For every two-letter word, give yourself two points. For every three-letter word, give yourself three points, and so on. Here's one to start you off:

nod

✻ QUIZ ANSWERS ✻

1. Mistletoe
2. Sugar plums
3. Christmas pudding
4. Saint Nicholas
5. The Queen
6. It has to snow!
7. Meat, usually beef
8. Klaxon
9. A coin
10. Hans Christian Andersen
11. Ebenezer Scrooge
12. Six
13. Two turtle doves and a partridge in a pear tree
14. A star
15. 6th January
16. Oliver Cromwell
17. The United States
18. Holly and Ivy
19. Melchior, Balthazar and Caspar
20. *Little Women*

EM'S
CHRISTMAS

I thought it was going to be the best Christmas ever. I woke up very very early and sat up as slowly as I could, trying not to shake the bed. I didn't want to wake Vita or Maxie. I wanted to have this moment all to myself.

I wriggled down to the end of the bed, carefully edging round Vita. She always curled up like a little monkey, knees right under her pointed chin, so the hump that was her stopped halfway down the duvet. It was so dark I couldn't see at all, but I could feel.

My hand stroked three little woolly socks stretched to bursting point. They were tiny stripy socks, too small even for Vita. The joke was to see how many weeny presents could be stuffed inside.

Vita and Maxie appreciated Santa's sense of humour and left him a minute mince pie on a doll's tea-set plate and a thimbleful of wine, and wrote him teeny thank-you letters on pieces of paper no bigger than a postage stamp. Well, Vita couldn't fit her shaky pencil printing on such a tiny scrap but she wrote 'Dear Santa I love you and pleese leeve me lots and lots of little pressents from your speshal frend Vita' on a big piece of paper and then folded it up again and again. Maxie simply wrote a letter 'M' and a lot of wonky kisses.

I wrote a letter too, even though I was only pretending for Vita and Maxie's sake. I knew who filled the Christmas socks. I thought he was much more magical than any bearded old gent in a red gown.

I felt past the socks to the space underneath. My hand brushed three parcels wrapped in crackly paper and tied with silk ribbon. I felt their shapes, wondering which one was for me. There was a very small square hard parcel, a flat oblong package and a large unwieldy squashy one, very wide at one end. I hung further out of bed, trying to work out the peculiar shape. I wriggled a little too far and went scooting right over the end, landing on my head.

Maxie woke up and started shrieking.

'Ssh! Shut up, Maxie! It's OK, don't cry,' I said, crawling past the presents to Maxie's little mattress.

He doesn't want to sleep in a proper bed. He likes to set up a camp with lots of blankets and cushions and all his cuddly toys. Sometimes it's hard to spot Maxie himself under all his droopy old teddies.

I wrestled my way through a lot of fur and found

Maxie, quivering in his going-to-bed jersey and underpants. That's another weird thing about Maxie, he hates pyjamas. There are a lot of weird things about my little brother.

I crawled onto his mattress and cuddled him close. 'It's me, silly.'

'I thought you were a Wild Thing coming to get me,' Maxie sobbed.

Where the Wild Things Are was Dad's favourite book. The little boy in it is called Max, and he tames all these Wild Thing monsters. That's where our Maxie got his name. Reading the book to him was a big mistake. Our Maxie couldn't ever tame Wild Thing scary monsters. He wouldn't be up to taming wild fluffy baby bunnies.

'The Wild Things are all shut up in their book, Maxie,' I whispered. 'Stop crying, you'll make my nightie all wet. Cheer up, it's Christmas!'

'Is Father Christmas here?' Vita shouted, jumping out from under the duvet.

'Ssh! It's only six o'clock. But he's been, he's left us presents.'

'Has he left any presents for me?' said Maxie.

'No, none whatsoever,' said Vita, jumping down the bed and pouncing on the presents. 'Yay! For dear Vita, love from Santa. And here we are again – To darling Vita, even more love from Santa. And there's this one too, To my special sweetheart Vita, lots and lots and lots of love from Santa. Nothing for you two at all.'

Maxie started sobbing again.

'She's just teasing, Maxie. Don't let her wind you up. Shut up, Vita. Be nice, it's Christmas. Leave the presents alone. We open them in Mum and Dad's bed, you know we do.'

'Let's go to their room now!' said Vita, scrabbling at the bottom of the bed, scooping up all three parcels and clutching them to her chest.

'No, no, it's not time yet. Mum will be cross,' I said, unpeeling Maxie and jumping up to restrain Vita.

'My daddy won't be cross with me,' said Vita. I always hated it when she said my daddy. It was a mean Vita trick to remind me that he wasn't really my dad.

He always said he loved me just as much as Vita and Maxie. I hoped hoped hoped it was true, because I loved him more than anyone else in the whole world, even a tiny bit more than Mum. More than Vita and Maxie. Much more than Gran.

'We'd better wait until seven, Vita,' I said.

'No!'

'Half past six then. Mum and Dad were out till late last night, they'll be tired.'

'They won't be tired, it's Christmas! Stop being so boring, Em. You just want to boss me about all the time.'

It's almost impossible to boss Vita even though

she's years younger than me and literally half my size. She's the one who's done the bossing, ever since she could sit up in her buggy and shriek. It is a royal pain having a little sister like Vita. You have to learn to be dead crafty if you want to manage her.

'If you come and cuddle back into bed I'll tell you another Princess Vita story,' I said. 'A special Christmas Princess Vita story where she gets to fly to Santa's workshop and has the pick of all his presents. And she meets Mrs Christmas and all the little children Christmases – Clara Christmas, Caroline Christmas and little Charlie Christmas.'

'Can Prince Maxie play with Charlie Christmas?' said Maxie.

'No, he can't. This is my Princess Vita story,' said Vita.

I had her hooked. She got back into bed. Maxie grabbed an armful of teddies and climbed into our bed too. I lay between them, making up the story.

Princess Vita stories were very boring because they always had to be about sweetly pretty show-off Princess Vita. Everyone adored her and wanted to be her friend and gave her elaborate presents. I had to go into extreme detail describing each designer princess gown with matching wings, her jewelled ten-league trainers, and the golden crown the exact shade of Princess Vita's long long curls.

Our Vita wriggled and squirmed excitedly, and

when I started describing the golden crown (and the pink diamond tiara and the ruby slides and the amethyst hair bobbles) she tossed her head around as if she was adorning her own long long curls. She hasn't really got any. Vita has very thin, fine, straight baby hair like beige cotton. She's been growing it for several years but it still hasn't reached her shoulders.

My hair is straw rather than mouse, and thick and strong. When I undo my plaits it very nearly reaches my waist (if I tilt my head right back).

'Please put Prince Maxie into the story,' Maxie begged, nuzzling his head against my neck. His hair is the same length as Vita's, coal-black with a long fringe. If he's wriggled around a lot in the night it sticks straight out like a chimney brush.

'Princess Vita has a brother called Prince Maxie, the boldest biggest boy in the whole kingdom,' I said.

Maxie sucked in his breath with pleasure.

'As if!' said Vita. 'Bother Prince Maxie. Tell about Princess Vita's trip to see Santa.'

I ended up telling two stories, swerving from one to the other, five minutes of Princess Vita, a quick diversion to see Prince Maxie defeating the seven-headed dragon spouting scarlet flames, and then back to Princess Vita's sortie in Santa's sleigh.

'There aren't really seven-headed dragons, are there?' said Maxie.

 256

'No, you've killed the very last one,' I said.

'How do you know there aren't any more hiding in their caves?' Maxie asked.

'Oh yes, there are lots and lots, all huddled down in the dark so you can't see them, but they come creeping out at night all ready to get you,' Vita said gleefully.

'Will you stop being so mean to him, you bad girl!' I said. 'I'll torture you!' I got hold of her stick wrist and gave her a tiny Chinese burn.

'Didn't hurt,' Vita laughed. 'No one can hurt me. I'm Princess Vita. If any monsters come bothering me I'll give them one kick with my ten-league trainers and they'll beg for mercy.'

'OK, let's get you begging for mercy. I'm going to tickle you,' I said, scrabbling under her chin, in her armpit, on her tummy.

Vita giggled and kicked and squirmed, trying to burrow under the duvet away from me.

'Come on, Maxie, let's get her,' I said.

'Tickle tickle tickle,' said Maxie, his hands shaped into little claws. He stabbed at Vita ineffectively. She was in such a giggly heap she squealed anyway.

'I'm tickling Vita!' Maxie said proudly.

'Yeah, look, she's cowering away from you,' I said. 'But there's no escape, little Vita, the tickle torturers are relentless.'

I reached right under the duvet and found her

feet. I held one captive with one hand and tickled the other.

'No, no, stop it, you beast!' Vita screamed, thrashing and kicking.

'Hey, hey, who's being murdered?' Dad came into the room, hands on his hips, just wearing his jeans.

'Dad!' We all three yelled his name and jumped at him for a big hug. 'Merry Christmas, Dad!'

'Santa's been, Dad, look!'

'He left lots of presents – all for me!' said Vita.

'You wish, little Vita,' said Dad. He caught her up and whirled her round and round.

'Me too, me too,' Maxie begged.

'No, little Maxie, we're going to toss you like a pancake,' said Dad, picking Maxie up and hurling him high in the air. Maxie shrieked in terror, but bore it because he didn't want to be left out.

I didn't want to be left out either but I knew there was no way Dad could whirl or toss me. I sat back on the bed feeling larger and lumpier than ever. Dad pretended to take a bite out of Maxie pancake and then set him free. Dad smiled at me.

He bowed formally.

'Would you care to dance, Princess Glittering Green Emerald?'

I jumped up and Dad started doing this crazy jive with me, singing a rock 'n' roll version of 'Rudolph the

 258

Red-Nosed Reindeer'. Vita and Maxie started jumping around too, Vita light as a feather, Maxie thumping.

'Hey, hey, calm down now, kids, we'll wake Mum.'

'We want to wake Mum,' said Vita. 'We want our presents!'

'OK, let's go and wish her happy Christmas,' said Dad. 'Bring the presents into our room.'

'They aren't really all for Vita, are they, Dad?' said Maxie.

'There's one each for all of you,' said Dad. 'That one is for my number one son.'

'I'm your number one daughter, aren't I, Dad?' said Vita, elbowing me out of the way.

'You're my special little daughter,' said Dad.

I waited. I didn't want to be his big daughter.

'You're my special grown-up daughter, Emerald,' said Dad.

My name isn't really Emerald, it's plain Emily. All the rest of the family called me Em. I loved it when Dad called me Emerald.

'Shall I go and make you and Mum a cup of tea?' I offered.

I loved being treated like a grown-up too. Vita and Maxie weren't allowed anywhere near the cooker and couldn't so much as switch on the kettle.

'That would be great, darling, but if you start faffing around in the kitchen your gran will wake up.'

'Ah. Right.' We certainly didn't want Gran climbing into Mum and Dad's bed with us.

'Come on then, kids. Let's get the Christmas show on the road,' said Dad. He yawned and ran his fingers through his long hair. My dad's got the most beautiful long hair in the whole world. It's thick and dark and glossy black, like Maxie's, but Dad's grown his way past his shoulders. He wears it in one tight fat plait during the day to keep it neat, and then it's all lovely and loose at night. It looks so strange and special, so perfect for Dad. He gets fed up with it sometimes, saying he looks like some silly old hippy, and he's always threatening to get it cut.

That's how Dad met Mum. He went into her hairdressing salon at the top of the Pink Palace on the spur of the moment and asked her to chop it all off. She took one look at him and said no way.

She said she didn't usually go for guys with long hair but said it really suited Dad and it would be a shame to spoil such a distinctive look. That's what she said. I knew this story off by heart. Dad liked her paying him compliments so he asked her if she'd come for a drink with him when she finished work. They ended up spending the whole evening together and falling madly in love. They've been together ever since. Just like a fairy story. They don't live in an enchanted castle because Mum doesn't earn that much money as a hairdresser and Dad earns less as an actor, though he has his fairy stall at the Pink Palace now. He works very hard, no matter what Gran says.

We tiptoed along the landing so as not to wake her. She has the biggest bedroom at the front. I suppose that's only fair as it's her house, but it means Mum and Dad are squashed up in the little bedroom, and Vita, Maxie and me are positively crammed into our room. Gran suggested one of us might like to go and sleep in her room with her but we thought that was a terrible idea.

Gran snores for a start. We could hear her snoring on Christmas morning even though her bedroom door was shut. Dad gave a very tiny piggy snore, imitating her, and we all got the giggles. We had to hold our hands over our mouths to muffle them (not easy clutching Christmas stockings and slippery parcels!). We exploded into Mum and Dad's bedroom, dropping everything, jumping on the bed, snorting with laughter.

Mum sat up, startled, her hair hanging in her eyes. 'What . . . ?' she mumbled.

'Merry Christmas, Mum!'

'Happy Christmas, babe,' said Dad, kissing her.

'Oh darling, happy happy Christmas,' said Mum, flinging her arms round him and running her fingers through his hair.

 261

'Give me a Christmas kiss, Mum!' Vita demanded, pulling at her bare shoulder.

'Me too,' said Maxie.

'Me too, me too, me too!' I said, making a joke of it, sending them up.

'Happy Christmas, kids. Big big kisses for all of you in just a minute,' said Mum, wrapping her dressing gown round her and climbing out of bed.

'Hey, where are you going?' said Dad, climbing back in. 'Come back!'

'Got to take a little trip to the bathroom, darling,' said Mum.

We couldn't be mean enough to start opening our stockings without her. She kept us waiting a little while. She came back smelling of toothpaste and her special rosy soap, her face powdered, her hair teased and sprayed into her usual blonde bob.

'Come on, babe, come and cuddle up,' said Dad, hitching Vita and Maxie along to make room for her.

He ruffled Mum's hair like she was a little kid too. Mum didn't moan, even though she'd just made it perfect. She waited until Dad was helping Maxie with his stocking and then she quickly patted her hair back into shape, smoothing down her fringe and tweaking the ends. She wasn't being vain. She was just trying extra hard to look nice for Dad.

We had this tradition of opening presents in turn,

starting with the youngest, but this wasn't such a good idea with Maxie. He was so slow, delicately picking out the first tiny parcel from his stocking, prodding it warily and then cautiously shaking it, as if he thought it might be a miniature bomb. When he decided it was safe to open he spent ages nudging the edge of the sellotape with his thumbnail.

'Hurry up, Maxie,' Vita said impatiently. 'Just pull the paper.'

'I don't want to rip it, it looks so pretty. I want to wrap all my presents up again after I've seen what they are,' said Maxie.

'Here, son, let me help,' said Dad, and within a minute or two he'd shelled all Maxie's stocking presents out of their shiny paper.

Maxie cupped his hands to hold them all at once: his magic pencil that could draw red and green and blue and yellow all in one go; a silver spiral notebook; a weeny yellow plastic duck no bigger than his thumb; a tiny toy tractor; a mini box of Smarties; a little watch on a plastic strap; a green glass marble; and a pair of his very own nail clippers (Maxie always wants to borrow Dad's).

'How does Santa know exactly what I like?' said Maxie.

'How indeed?' said Dad solemnly.

'Will you help me wrap them all up now, Dad?'

'Yeah, of course I will.'

'I'm unwrapping mine!' said Vita, spilling her goodies all over the duvet, ripping each one open with her scrabbly little fingers. She found a tiny pink lady ornament in a ballet frock; sparkly butterfly hairslides; a set of kitten and puppy stickers; a miniature red box of raisins; a weeny purple brush and comb set; a little book about a rabbit with print so tiny you could hardly read it; a bead necklace spelling I LOVE VITA; and her very own real lipstick.

'I hope Santa's given you a very pale pink lipstick,' said Mum. 'Go on then, Em, open your stocking.'

I was getting too big to believe in Santa but he still wanted to please me. I found a little orange journal with its own key; a tiny red heart soap; a purple gel pen; cherry bobbles for my hair; a tiny tin of violet sweets; a Miffy eraser; a Jenna Williams bookmark; and a small pot of silver glitter nail varnish.

'I love that colour,' said Mum. 'Santa's got good taste, Em. I wish he'd leave me a stocking.'

'You've got our presents, Mum,' I said.

They weren't really special enough. We always made our presents for Mum and Dad, and so they looked like rubbish. Maxie did a drawing of Mum and Dad and Vita and me, but we weren't exactly recognizable. We looked like five potatoes on toothpicks.

Vita did a family portrait too. She drew herself

very big, her head touching one end of the paper and her feet the other. She embellished herself with very long thick hair and silver shoes with enormously high heels. She drew Dad one side of her, Mum the other, using up so much space she had to squash Maxie and me high up in either corner, just our heads and shoulders, looking down like gargoyles.

I felt I was too old for drawing silly pictures. I wanted to make them proper presents. Gran had recently taught me to knit, so at the beginning of December I'd started to knit a woollen patchwork quilt for Mum and Dad's bed. I knitted and knitted and knitted – in the playground, watching television, on the loo – but by Christmas Eve I had only managed eleven squares, not even enough for a newborn baby's quilt.

I sewed the prettiest pink square into a weird pouch done up with a pearly button. It was too holey for a purse but I thought Mum could maybe keep her comb inside. I sewed the other ten squares into one long scarf for Dad. It wasn't exactly the right shape and it rolled over at the edges but I hoped he might still like it.

'I absolutely love it, Em,' he said, wrapping it round his neck. 'I've wanted a long stripy scarf ever since I watched Dr Who when I was a little kid. Thank you, darling.' He stroked the uneven rows. 'It's so cosy! I'll be as warm as toast all winter.'

I felt my cheeks glowing. I knew he probably hated it and didn't want to be seen dead wearing it, but he made me believe he truly loved it at the same time.

Mum gave him a V-necked soft black sweater and he put it on at once, but he kept my scarf round his neck.

'What about my present?' Mum asked, as eagerly as Vita.

'What present?' said Dad, teasing her. Then he reached underneath the bed and handed her an oblong package. She felt the parcel and then tore off the wrapping. A pair of silver shoes tumbled out, strappy sandals with the highest heels ever.

'Oh my God!' Mum shrieked. 'They're so beautiful. Oh darling, how wicked, how glamorous, how incredible!' She started kissing Dad rapturously.

'Hey, hey, they're just shoes,' he said. 'Come on then, kids, open your big presents.'

He helped Maxie unwrap an enormous set of expensive Caran d'Ache colouring pens and a big white pad of special artist's paper.

'But he's just a little kid, Frankie. He'll press too hard and ruin the tips,' Mum said.

'No I won't, Mum!' said Maxie.

'He will,' I mouthed at Mum. Maxie had already totally ruined the red and the sky-blue in my set of felt pens. I couldn't help feeling envious of Maxie's beautiful set, so superior to my own.

'My turn, my turn, my turn!' Vita shouted, tearing at her huge parcel. One weird long brown twisty thing poked through the paper as she scrabbled at it, then another.

'What is it?' Vita shrieked.

Then she discovered a big pink nose.

'Is it a clown?' Maxie asked fearfully.

Dad had taken us to the circus in the summer and Maxie had spent most of the evening under his seat, terrified of the clowns.

'Try pressing that nose,' said Dad. Vita poked at it, and it played a pretty tinkly tune.

'That's "The Sugar Plum Fairy" from some ballet. We did it in music,' I said.

Vita tore the last of the paper away to reveal the huge sweet head of a furry reindeer, with two twisty plush antlers sticking out at angles. She had big brown glass eyes, fantastic long eyelashes, and a smiley red-lined mouth with a soft pink tongue. She was wearing a pink ballet dress with a satin bodice and net skirt.

'I love her, I love her!' Vita declared, hugging her passionately to her chest.

The reindeer had long floppy furry legs with pink satin ballet slippers, but she couldn't stand on them. I lifted the net skirt and saw a big hole.

'Don't look up her bottom!' Vita snapped.

'Um, Em's being rude,' said Maxie.

'No, I'm not! I've just realized, she's a glove puppet!'

'You got it, Emerald,' said Dad. 'Here, Vita, let's get to know her. We'll see if she'll introduce herself.' He pressed her pink nose again to stop the ballet music and stuck his hand up inside her.

'Hello, Princess Vita,' he made the reindeer say, in a funny fruity female voice. 'I'm Dancer. I was one of Santa's very own reindeers. Maybe you've heard of my fellow sleigh artistes, Dasher and Prancer and Vixen? Then there's the so-called superstar, Rudolph, the one with the constant cold. Such a show-off, especially since he got his own song. Of course I was always the leading runner, until I realized that all that sleigh-pulling wasn't such a good idea. I have very sensitive hooves. Santa was devastated when I gave in my notice but we artistes have to consider our talent. I am now Princess Vita's dancing companion and trusty steed.'

Dad made Dancer bow low and then twirl on her floppety legs. Vita clapped her hands, bright red with excitement.

I felt envious again. Why couldn't I have had a puppet? Then Dad and I could have had endless games together. Vita and Maxie had such special big presents this year. Why did mine have to be so tiny? It was just like one extra stocking present.

'Aren't you going to open your present, Emerald?' said Dad. He slipped Dancer over Vita's hand, showing her how to work her. Vita waved her wildly round and round. Maxie laughed and tried to catch Dancer. One of her antlers accidently poked him in the eye.

'Hey, hey, watch out! Oh Maxie, for heaven's sake, it didn't really hurt,' said Mum, grabbing Vita's arm and pulling Maxie close for a cuddle.

'Yes, Em, open your present. Whatever can it be?'

I undid the wrapping paper, feeling foolish with them all watching me. I got my mouth all puckered up, waiting to say thank you and give grateful kisses. Then I opened a little black box and stared at what was inside. I was stunned. I couldn't say anything at all.

'What is it, Em?'

'Show us!'

'Don't you like it?'

It was a little gold ring set with a deep green glowing jewel.

'I love it,' I whispered. 'It's an emerald!'

'Not a real emerald, darling,' said Mum.

'Yes it is,' said Dad. 'I'm not fobbing off my daughter with anything less!'

My daughter! I loved that almost as much as my beautiful ring.

'Don't be silly, Frankie,' Mum said. 'Real emeralds cost hundreds and hundreds of pounds!'

'No they don't. Not if you go to antique fairs and do

 269

someone a favour and find a little emerald for a special small girl,' said Dad.

He unhooked the ring from its little velvet cushion and put it on the ring finger of my right hand.

'It fits perfectly!' I said.

'Well, I had it made specially for you, Princess Emerald,' said Dad.

'But however much have you spent on all of us?' Mum said, shaking her head as if she'd been swimming underwater.

'Never you mind,' said Dad. 'I wanted this to be a special Christmas, one the kids will remember for ever.'

* CHRISTMAS AROUND * THE WORLD

Did you know . . .

- In Italy, children write letters to Babbo Natale, to tell him that they've been good throughout the year. But the main day for giving presents is Twelfth Night, or the start of Epiphany, January 6th – and traditionally, those gifts are supposed to be brought by a good witch called La Befana. Legend has it that La Befana brings sweets and other treats in the middle of the night, and then sweeps the floor with her broom before leaving!

- In Brazil, some children leave a sock near a window. If Papai Noel finds it, he'll swap it for a present!

- In France, the most important Christmas meal is called Reveillon, and it happens late on Christmas Eve or very early on Christmas Day, after people return home from Midnight Mass. A special chocolate log cake, called a Bûche de Noël, is often eaten.

- In the Czech Republic, the main Christmas meal also happens on Christmas Eve, but it's traditional to eat fish soup, followed by fried fish and potato salad.

- Norway gives the UK a very special Christmas present every year: an enormous Christmas tree. It's given as a thank you for the help that the UK gave to Norway during the Second World War, and it always stands in Trafalgar Square in London. There's a big ceremony when the lights are switched on!

- In Spain, December 28th is called Día de los Santos Inocentes or Day of the Innocent Saints, and is like April Fools' Day in the UK. People try to trick each other into believing silly stories and jokes, and even newspapers and TV programmes join in.

- In Germany, one tradition is for a small group of children – the Sternsinger, or star singers – to go from house to house, singing carols. Three dress up like the Wise Men, and one carries a star, as a symbol for the Star of Bethlehem.

- In Iceland, Gamlárskvöld – New Year's Eve – is considered a very special and magical night, where all sorts of strange things are rumoured to happen. Legend has it that cows can talk, seals take on human form and the elves move house!

CHARLIE'S CHRISTMAS

I went round to Jamie's house and hunted through the Victorian books – and found a great big fat one with lots of recipes called Mrs Beeton's Book of Household Management. I flipped through it until I found the perfect cake.

It needed quite a lot of ingredients but that was no problem. (For reasons I will divulge later!)

It took ages to make the special cake. I had to make this special lemon jelly and then pour a little bit into a big tin and then stud it with glacé cherries like jewels, and then I did another layer of jelly and stood sponge fingers all the way round the tin and then I made a special eggy custard and poured that on and let it all set and THEN the next day I dunked the tin very quickly in hot water and then, holding my breath and praying, I gently tipped it out onto a pretty plate like a little kid turning out a sandcastle. You

know what often happens with sandcastles? They crumble and break, right? But my special Victorian cake came out whole and perfect, easy-peasy, simple-pimple.

It was a bit of a mega-problem getting it to school, though. I had to carry it on a tray and hope it wouldn't rain. My arms were aching terribly by the time I got to school. I was a bit late too, because I'd had to walk so carefully to keep my cake intact.

'Charlotte Enright, you're late for school,' said Miss Beckworth.

'Only half a second, Miss Beckworth. And it's in a very very good cause,' I said, propping my heavy tray on a desk and peeling back the protective tinfoil I'd arched over it.

'And what's this very good cause, might I ask?' said Miss Beckworth.

'You!' I said, pulling the last of the foil off with a flourish. 'I've made you a cake, Miss Beckworth. Well, it's for all of us at the disco, but it's in your honour and you've got to have the first slice. It's a Victorian cake. And you'll never ever guess what it's called!'

Miss Beckworth looked at my wondrous masterpiece. She blinked her all-seeing eyes. They twinkled as she met my gaze.

'I can guess,' said Miss Beckworth. 'In your own ultra-irritating phrase, it's easy-peasy, simple-pimple!

It's an absolutely magnificent Charlotte Russe.'

She really is all-knowing! We shared the cake-cutting ceremony when it was nosh time.

I got a bit worried my Charlotte cake would collapse, but it stood its ground splendidly. And it tasted great too, mega-yummy. It was all gone in a matter of minutes – just a lick of lemon jelly and a few sponge crumbs left on the plate.

I made sure all my special friends got a slice. Then the disco started up. It wasn't a real evening disco with a proper DJ and strobe lighting. It was just an afternoon Christmas party in the school hall for Year Six, with the headmaster playing these mostly ropy old discs. Hardly the most sophisticated exciting event of the century – though you'd maybe think it was, judging by the fuss Lisa and Angela and some of the other girls made.

We were allowed to change into our own home clothes, you see. The boys didn't think it much of a big deal. They looked worse out of school uniform.

I didn't try too hard either. I was too busy creating my cake to fuss about my outfit. And I can't actually win when it comes to cool clothes way in the front line of fashion. My kit comes from the label-free zones of Oxfam, Jumble and Car Boot Sales, especially nowadays. Though this might change soon. (Second hint of changes in the Enright family fortunes!)

Lisa and Angela and lots of the other girls tried very hard indeed. Lisa looked particularly lovely.

But Angela was the big surprise. She usually wore ordinary old jeans and jumpers when we were hanging round after school. But now her mum had bought her this new party-time outfit down the market. Angela's got too tall for kids' clothes so this was really grown-up gear. And Angela looked ultra-adult in it too.

'Look at *Angela*!'

You couldn't help looking at her. Everyone did. It was as if she'd become an entirely new girl to match her new outfit. When she danced the boys all circled round. Even Dave Wood.

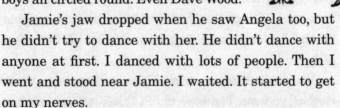

Jamie's jaw dropped when he saw Angela too, but he didn't try to dance with her. He didn't dance with anyone at first. I danced with lots of people. Then I went and stood near Jamie. I waited. It started to get on my nerves.

'Come on, Jamie. Let's dance,' I said commandingly.

'I don't think I'm very good at dancing,' said Jamie.

He was right about that. He just stood and twitched a little at first.

'Let yourself go a bit,' I said, jumping about. Jamie let himself go a bit too much. His arms and legs

shot out all over the place. I had to
stay well back to stop myself getting
clouted. But I suppose he was trying.

Lisa was standing near us. I prepared myself for some ultra-sarcastic
comments. But Lisa's eyes were a little too bright, her
smile showing too much teeth. She wasn't watching
Jamie and me. She was watching Angela and Dave.

'Hey, Jamie. I want to dance with Lisa for a bit,' I said.

'Good! I need a rest,' Jamie puffed.

So I danced with Lisa for a bit. And then I danced
with some of the other girls. And some other boys. So
did Lisa. And at long last Dave Wood came slithering
up to her, because he'd been elbowed away from Angela
by the rest of the boys. I expected Lisa to send Dave
Wood off with a flea in his ear. I'd have added a swarm
of stinging wasps and a buzz of killer bees. But would
you believe it, Lisa just gave him this stupid smirk
and danced with him devotedly. Lisa has got a very
pretty head but it contains no brain whatsoever.

'Do you want to dance again, Charlie?' Jamie asked
eagerly. 'I think I'm getting the hang of it now.'

He was a little optimistic. But we had fun all the
same. The party ended at three and we were allowed
to go home then.

Lisa and Dave Wood went off together,
so she was happy.

Angela went off with half the boys in our class,  so she was happy. I decided to go back to Jamie's house because I was still a bit peckish in spite of my Charlotte Russe (the other refreshments weren't up to much) and I fancied one of his brother's toasted cheese sandwiches. We walked along Oxford Terrace together. I peered up at all the attic rooms right under the roofs and imagined Lottie looking out.

Jamie kept walking closer and closer to me, so that his schoolbag banged my shins several times. I turned to tell him off – and he kissed me on the cheek!

'What are you playing at?' I said furiously.

'I – I – well, you kept sticking your chin up and looking up in the air so I thought you wanted me to kiss you,' Jamie stammered.

'Well, you got it seriously wrong, matie,' I said, giving him a shove. I scrubbed at the little wet patch on my cheek with the back of my hand. 'You do that again and I'll clock you one,' I said.

'Don't worry, I won't,' said Jamie. He sighed. 'I wish I could figure girls out. I especially wish I could figure you out, Charlie.'

'It's part of my deeply mysterious feminine charm,' I said, chuckling.

Jamie's brother came up trumps with another

toasted sandwich and his mum asked if Jo and I could go round to their house on Boxing Day. They have a party every year. Jo got a bit worried when I told her and said she didn't think it sounded her cup of tea – well, glass of punch – but she's agreed to come with me because I've been astonishingly agreeable about her Christmas plans.

I shall give Jamie his Christmas present then. I've bought him a big fat paperback Victorian novel. *Jane Eyre* – by Charlotte Brontë, and inside the cover I've written: *This is a present by a Charlotte, from a Charlotte!*

I'm going to make Jamie's mum a special cake to eat at her party. I've got it all worked out. It's going to

be a square cake, iced all over with a cake lid on top and marzipan ribbon, so it looks like a special gift box – for Boxing Day, get it? I'm going to be so busy busy busy making cakes in the Christmas holidays. I've got to make one for Grandma and Grandpa when Jo and I go over there on Christmas Eve – yuck! I had all sorts of good ideas but Jo talked it over with me and she thinks they'd like an ordinary conventional Christmas cake, white icing and HAPPY CHRISTMAS, boring boring boring – but I've said I'll do it.

I'm making one more cake – and this one's a special one.

Jo fixed a beautiful red breakfast in bed for us on Sunday (ruby grapefruit and raspberry Danish pastries and cranberry juice). When we'd eaten it all up we cuddled down in bed again and I started up one of our games and Jo tried to join in but I could tell she wasn't concentrating.

'Jo? What is it, eh?' I could feel her tense.

'Well . . . I want to talk to you about something,' she said.

I felt as if all the delicious red food inside me was being whisked in a blender. This was it. I knew what she was going to say. I wriggled away from her and lay stiffly in bed, waiting.

'It's about . . . Robin,' she said.

'And Mark,' I said, through clenched teeth.

'Well. Yes, I suppose so. Oh, Charlie. I don't know how to say this.'

'I'll say it for you,' I said. 'It's easy-peasy, simple-pimple. You and Mark are going to get married and Robin's going to be my little brother and you'll be giving up all your jobs to look after him full-time and we'll have to sell our flat and go and live with them and I expect you want me to make you a flipping wedding

cake as well, but if I have to come to your wedding I warn you, I won't throw confetti, I'll start throwing rocks at you,' and I turned over on my tummy and started to cry.

'What?' said Jo. 'What?' And she started to laugh.

'It's not funny!' I sobbed. 'I want to stay here. With you. Just the two of us.'

'So do I,' said Jo. She shoved my tangled hair out of the way and said it straight into my ear. 'So do I! That's what we're going to do. Now listen, Charlie! You've got it all wrong. Mark and I aren't getting married. He's still too fussed about his first marriage – and I don't think I ever want to get married. OK?'

'So you don't love him?'

'I don't know what I feel. I just want to let things develop. Slowly. In their own time. I hope I'll still see a lot of Mark and Robin – but I might not carry on working there. You know this Christmas job?'

You don't know about the Christmas job. Jo's stopped working at the Rosens'. The last big electrical goods shop in the town advertised for part-time staff to help them out over their busy Christmas trading time. Jo jumped in there and they took her on right away, working from nine to three. So we've got enough to keep up the mortgage payments – and a bit over. That's what I was hinting at earlier.

'You mean it's too tiring, working there and then going to look after Robin?' I said, leaning up on my elbows.

'The thing is, the shop manageress is going to have a baby. She wants to start her maternity leave in

283

January – and even though I'm only temporary they're asking if I'm interested. It won't be for ever, of course, though she might decide she wants to stay at home with the baby – but it would still be great to get back to the work I like. But of course it would be full time, through till half past five.'

'I see. Well. You'll have to take it, Jo. I mean, it's great. But . . . what about Robin? He likes you a lot.'

'He likes you even more, Charlie. Mark hopes he'll be able to juggle his working hours and pick Robin up from school himself. Or maybe he'll have to find another child-minder. But in an absolute emergency I said you could always pick Robin up from school and look after him until Mark could come.'

'Mark wouldn't ever trust me with Robin!' I said.

'Yes he would. He knows that you're really very sensible and responsible,' said Jo.

'Me?' I said. 'OK. Tell Mark he can count on me. As long as he pays me!'

'Charlie!'

'So we can really stay here in our own flat, Jo?'

'You bet.'

'And we'll have our first Christmas here, just us two?'

'Ah. Well. That's the other thing I wanted to discuss.'

This time I did guess right.

'You want Robin and Mark to come round here for Christmas?'

'If that's all right with you, Charlie?'

I didn't want Mark to come at all. Still, it might be fun to have Robin bobbing about at Christmas. So . . . I decided I'd better come up with something pretty special for our Christmas cake. I baked a square fruit cake and then carved out part of the front and made up a brown butter icing and did this posh basket weave all over to make it look like . . . a stable! With a big gold marzipan star and a fat pink marzipan angel perched on the roof. (I'm going to get to eat the angel on Christmas Day – because I'm currently so angelic!) Then I made a marzipan Mary (Jo can eat her) and a marzipan Joseph (I suppose I might offer him to Mark) and a dear little marzipan baby Jesus clutching a white marzipan lamb (specially for Robin).

I piped a long message in front of all my Nativity figures.

PEACE ON EARTH. GOOD WILL TO ALL MEN.

I never ever thought I'd be wishing Good Will to any man! I decided to add a bit.

AND GOOD WILL TO ALL WOMEN AND BOYS AND ESPECIALLY GIRLS!

* · * · * · * · * · * · * · * · *

* CHARLIE'S CHRISTMAS CAKE *

There are lots of ingredients and lots of steps involved when making a real Christmas cake, so you might want to ask for some help – and you'll need plenty of time! Try to make your cake a few weeks before Christmas, and keep it wrapped up tightly in foil or a cake tin until you're ready to eat it.

For your cake:
- 225g plain flour
- ½ tsp mixed spice
- ½ tsp ground cinnamon
- 200g butter
- 200g dark brown sugar
- 2 tbsp black treacle
- ½ tsp vanilla essence
- 4 large eggs
- 700g mixed dried fruit (choose whatever you like best – sultanas, raisins, apricots and cranberries are all delicious!)
- 100g chopped mixed peel
- 150g chopped nuts
- 100ml strong tea

For your topping:
- 200g marzipan
- 2 tbsp apricot jam

* · * · * · * · * · * · * · * · *

What to do:

1. Heat the oven to 150°C. Grease a 20cm round cake tin and line the bottom and sides with baking parchment.

2. Put the flour, mixed spice and cinnamon into a bowl.

3. Put the butter and the sugar in a separate mixing bowl and then add the sugar, treacle and vanilla essence, and beat until light and fluffy.

4. Mix the eggs one at a time into the mixture.

5. Fold in the flour mixture, then mix in the dried fruit, mixed peel and nuts.

6. Tip the mixture into the prepared tin and bake in the oven for 3 hours, until a metal skewer pushed into the centre of the cake comes out clean.

7. Remove from the oven and leave to cool in the tin for 15 minutes. Then turn out on to a wire rack and leave to cool fully.

8. Once cool, make a few little holes in the cake with a skewer and pour the tea over the top very carefully, so the liquid soaks into the cake.

9. When you're ready to decorate the cake, place the cake on a foil board or cake plate. Dust your hands and the work surface with a little icing sugar and knead the marzipan until soft. Roll out half the marzipan to fit the top of the cake and roll out the rest in strips to fit around the sides of the cake. Brush the cake all over with the warmed apricot jam and then place the marzipan on top and around the cake.

10. A week or so before Christmas, you could add white icing too!

HAPPY
NEW YEAR

Wednesday 1st January

Happy New Year! No, more like *Unhappy* New Year.

I don't know what to write in this silly diary. Nan gave it to me as part of my Christmas present.

'You want to be a writer, don't you, Milly?' she said.

Well, yes, I *do* want to be a writer, but I don't want to write about my own boring dreary horrible life. I want to write about a wonderful fantasy Millyland where I'm the princess and I get to do everything I want and I can have all the animals I fancy, especially gerbils, and I live in my own palace and make as much noise as I care to and nobody ever tells me off.

I don't live in a palace now. I don't live in my own house any more. I have to live with my nan and grandad. I don't even have my own bedroom, I have to share with my mum.

We live here because Dad left us last summer and we couldn't stay in our house because we hadn't paid the rent. Nan says, 'Never mind, we'll get along fine, our own special family of four.' She had to nudge Grandad hard to make him back her up. I don't think he's very keen on this arrangement. Actually I don't think he's very keen on me.

He's a policeman and he's used to telling people what to do – so at home he bosses Nan around and he bosses Mum and he particularly bosses me. He does shift work so he is sometimes asleep during the day. I don't always remember this and I dash up the stairs or I slam a door or I turn on the television and then he yells crossly, 'Tell that kid to pipe down, I'm trying to have a kip!'

He's asleep now because he was on duty all last night. Mum's asleep too. She went to some neighbour's New Year's party up the road. I didn't get to go anywhere. I'm not that friendly with any of the children in my class at this new school just yet. I didn't want to go out anyway because I hoped my dad would ring me to wish me a Happy New Year.

He didn't. He *did* send me the most amazing

Christmas presents though – an iPhone 5, would you believe, and a pair of leather boots with heels (OK, only little ones) and a real silver charm bracelet. Mum got upset because she could only afford to get me a little present this year and Nan got upset because she said I was much too young to have a smartphone and heeled boots and real jewellery. Grandad got upset too, and said Dad should pay Mum proper maintenance and not waste his money.

I didn't get the slightest bit upset. I love my Dad. I miss him sooooo much. I miss Gilbert too. He was my very special beautiful little boy gerbil and I loved him desperately. I especially loved letting him scurry down my school blouse and nestle on top of my tummy. It used to drive Nan nuts when she came on a visit. She's seriously weird. She's *scared* of gerbils. So I had to give Gilbert away when we came to live at her house. It was one of the saddest days of my life.

I'm still sad now. It's not going to be a Happy New Year.

Thursday 2nd January

Dad still hasn't rung. Mum's in a surprisingly good mood though. She's been a bit fed up and weepy for ages, but now she's all bouncy and she put on all her makeup and her best blue dress even though she was just going to work at her new waitressing job. Nan had to go to work at her dress shop so it was just Grandad and me at home.

Grandad was asleep all morning because he's still on nights. The morning was very l-o-n-g. And *boring*. I tried phoning Dad a few times with my new iPhone but he just had his answerphone message taking the calls. I phoned the message deliberately just to hear Dad's voice. 'Hi, you're through to Dave. Leave me a message and I'll get back to you.' So I left Dad some messages. *Lots* of messages.

Grandad came downstairs about one o'clock and caught me leaving yet another message.

'That's not a toy, Milly. You mustn't phone on a whim. You've got to have something to say,' he said.

'But I've got lots and lots to say to my Dad,' I said mournfully.

Grandad snorted. He can't stand my Dad, especially now. But he must have felt sorry for me because he offered to take me out to lunch. Normally we just have baked beans or pizzas at home as neither of us are great cooks.

'We'll go and check out your mum's restaurant, shall we?' he said.

'Oooh, yes!' I love eating there because Mum and all the other waitresses make a big fuss of me, and I get a specially big portion of chips and extra cream on my fruit pie.

So we went off together, Grandad and me, and we had a lovely lunch, and I had a banana toffee milkshake which was wonderful. Mum larked about a bit, and called me Miss Milly and treated me like a grown-up but she didn't act like she was actually listening all the time. She kept running to chat to this man sitting right at the other end by the serving hatch. I couldn't see him properly because his back was to me, but he must have been ordering a lot of food because he kept Mum talking for ages. She was obviously very hot from all the rushing about because she was bright pink.

Friday 3rd January

I know who that man is now. Mum told me last night. He's called Michael Everill and he lives near my nan's and he was at that New Year's party on Tuesday night. And Mum's going out with him tonight! On a date! I can't believe it. My mum! She's not a teenager. What about my dad?

I said all this, very fiercely indeed.

'You know your dad and I are divorced now, Milly. Michael's very nice and if – if we start going out together properly then you'll get to know him and I'm sure you'll like him,' said Mum.

'I won't like him. I'll loathe him,' I said.

'Now then, young lady, that's no way to talk to your mother,' said Grandad sternly.

'But it's disgusting, Mum going out with a strange man!' I said.

'He's not strange, dear. I've known the Everills for years. In fact he went to the very same primary school as your mum, though they were in different years,' said Nan.

'So he's much older than Mum?' I said.

'He's actually a year or two younger,' said Mum.

'So he's a toy boy!' I shrieked.

'I've told you once, watch your tongue!' said Grandad.

'That's not a very nice term, dear,' said Nan.

Mum said nothing at all. She was pink in the face again.

'Maybe – maybe seeing Michael isn't such a good idea,' she mumbled. 'It's early days and I don't want to get Milly all upset. I'll tell Michael I can't make it.'

'You'll do no such thing,' said Grandad. 'You'll go and enjoy yourself, dear. You can't tiptoe around worrying about upsetting Milly. You're going to turn her into a right little madam. And it's about time you went out with a decent bloke, after wasting so much time with that scoundrel.'

'My dad's not a scoundrel! You're a mean stupid fat pig to say such a thing!' I yelled.

I got sent to bed in disgrace. I'm writing my diary sitting up in bed now. I hate Grandad. I hate Nan too. And I hate Mum because she is still out on this awful date with this horrible Michael guy.

I love my Dad.

Later

I hate my Dad too. He rang me on my iPhone and I was so thrilled to hear his voice, but he just went on and on telling me off for leaving all the messages. He said he wasn't made of money and the phone was to be used very sparingly and anyway I must never ever phone him when he was at work.

'So when can I phone you, Dad?' I said, trying not to cry.

'In the evenings – I'm free then,' sad Dad.

But he wasn't free. I could hear music in the background, and then this woman's voice said, 'Supper's ready, darling.'

Dad has this girlfriend, Eva.

I hate her too.

I hate everyone.

Saturday 4th January

Mum didn't come home till very late last night. She hummed softly to herself as she took her clothes off and got into bed.

'Are you awake, Milly?' she whispered.

I kept my lips buttoned. I didn't want to say a single word to her. In fact I resolved not to speak to her ever again.

I kept it up at breakfast time the next morning. I didn't even say thank you when Mum made waffles for a special treat. Mum sighed, and made herself another cup of coffee.

'OK, Milly, we've got a whole Saturday together – it's my weekend off. Grandad's sleeping, and Nan's out at work all day. What would you like to do?'

I bent my head and stared fiercely at my plate. I said nothing.

'We can go out and have fun – or you can sit here sulking all day long. It's up to you,' said Mum.

I pondered. 'What are you doing this evening?' I mumbled. 'I bet you're going out with your boyfriend.'

Mum swallowed. 'He's not my boyfriend – not yet, anyway. And yes, I am seeing Michael. We're going to the pictures.'

'Oh, that's not fair – you promised to take me!' I wailed. 'I want to see that new funny film about animals!'

'I know. Michael and I are going to see a romance about a new couple and their problem children,' said Mum. 'Maybe I should have made the film myself! But if you like I'll take you to the animal film this afternoon as a special treat – even though you don't deserve one.'

 299

I hesitated. It wasn't really much fun being angry with Mum. I rushed to her all of a sudden and gave her a big hug and she sat me on her lap as if I was still little.

'That's my girl,' she said, rocking me.

'I don't like this Michael, Mum,' I said.

'I know. But I do.'

'As much as Dad?'

'Oh goodness, it's early days yet! Michael's just a friend. But a very sweet one. He's had a bit of a tough time, you know. His wife went off with someone else a year ago. He's got joint custody of their children. There's a girl about your age and a younger brother.'

'Do you know them?'

'No, I've never met them – but maybe . . . maybe tomorrow we could all meet up for Sunday lunch?' Mum suggested.

'But we always have Sunday lunch here, with Nan and Grandad!' I protested.

'Well, we don't have to. It's just a suggestion,' said Mum. 'Now, I'm still in a cooking mood. Want to do some baking?'

'Oh yes, please!' I said, because it's one of my favourite things to do, especially if I get to lick out the bowls afterwards. Mum and I made cupcakes with lots of pink buttercream and then a chocolate sponge with a chocolate frosting topping. I licked the bowls so clean they hardly needed to go in the dishwasher.

Grandad joined us for lunch and we had a healthy tuna salad for our first course – and then wonderfully naughty cupcakes for pudding!

Mum asked Grandad if he wanted to come with us to the cinema but he said he'd sooner watch the sport on television. He gave Mum ten pounds though to go towards the cinema tickets.

I knew Mum didn't really want to go and see the animal film, especially as she was going back to the cinema in the evening with *him*. She was just going to be kind to me.

I hadn't really been very kind to Mum.

I loved the animal film and roared with laughter. It felt good. I hadn't laughed very much for ages. I felt in such a good mood afterwards that I linked arms with Mum on the way home.

'Thanks for taking me, Mum,' I said. I paused. 'Sorry I was a bit mean to you this morning.'

'That's OK, Milly. It must feel a bit weird, having your mum go out on a date. I know just how much you still love your dad and you miss him terribly. He'll still always be

your father, you know. No one can ever replace him. You know that, don't you.'

I do know that. Dad phoned me when we got home, and we talked for ages and quite soon I'm going to stay with him for the weekend. Maybe next week. It will be great. I love love love my dad.

And I love my mum too.

Sunday 5th January 2014

Mum came back late last night too. I decided to talk to her this time.

'Did you have a good time?'

'Yes I did,' said Mum, a little cautiously.

'This Michael's still lovely, is he?' I said.

'Well.' Mum giggled. 'I think so.'

'Is he as good looking as Dad?'

'Mmm – no. He's more friendly-looking than hand-some.'

'Does he earn lots of money like Dad does now?'

'Nope. He works in a bookshop and doesn't get paid much at all – but he loves his job even so.'

'So he doesn't have a flash car like Dad?'

'He doesn't have any car at all.'

'So what's so special about him?' I asked.

'He's sweet and kind and funny and he makes me feel good,' said Mum.

'Oh.' That shut me up for a bit.

'And you can meet him yourself tomorrow. For Sunday lunch?' said Mum.

'I'll think about it,' I said.

I thought about it on and off all night. And this morning at breakfast (waffles again, yum!) I said casually, 'OK then – let's go to lunch at this Michael's.'

'You're sure?' said Mum. 'You – you will be polite to him, won't you?'

'I should blooming well hope she's polite!' said Grandad. 'You mollycoddle that kid far too much.'

'Now now,' said Nan, who always tries to keep the peace.

'I *milly*coddle her,' said Mum, laughing.

That made me giggle too. I felt OK for most of the morning – but when it was time to leave I suddenly felt totally weird. I didn't want to meet this Michael after all. I especially didn't want to see him and Mum together. What if they acted all lovey-dovey? It made me feel sick just thinking about it. And what were these children of his going to be like? I imagined a really horrid girl who might tease me and call me names. Some of the girls in my class at my new school were like that. It was awful being a new girl. I had heaps of friends at my

old school. The little brother would be just as bad – maybe even worse.

'I've changed my mind, Mum. I don't want to come,' I said, as Mum put our lovely chocolate cake in a fancy tin.

'Too late, lovie. I phoned to say we're coming,' said Mum.

'Yes, but I don't want to now,' I whined.

'I know. But I think you'll have fun when you get there. So we're going.'

'Are you giving them our chocolate cake?' I asked indignantly.

'We'll all have a slice for pudding,' said Mum.

I saw this Michael and his children having HUGE slices, so there was hardly any cake left for me. It made me hate them even more.

But then we got to Michael's. He lived in a flat, not a house, and it was a bit scruffy and untidy, with lots of books everywhere. He was a bit scruffy and untidy too, and nowhere near as handsome as my Dad – but I suppose he did look friendly. But thank goodness he wasn't all over me, not trying to hug me or anything – and he just said 'Hi' to Mum and didn't try to kiss her.

'It's lovely to meet you, Milly,' he said. 'You look just like your Mum – in other words, pretty stunning.'

Both Mum and I groaned, because this sounded

very cheesy – but I couldn't help hoping he meant it. No one has ever called me pretty stunning before, not even Dad.

'I knew what you looked like, sort of, because I saw the back of you in my mum's restaurant the other day,' I said.

'I don't know which is worse – my back view or my front!' said Michael. 'I love going to your mum's restaurant in my lunch hour. The service is delightful!'

'I bet you get banana toffee milkshakes made especially for you,' I said.

'I don't. You clearly get preferential treatment,' said Michael.

'Where are your children?' I said. 'I thought they were going to be here too?'

'They're in my bedroom, watching some film on my old portable telly,' said Michael.

'Why don't you go and say hello, Milly, while I give Michael a hand in the kitchen?' said Mum.

I really didn't want to. Michael didn't seem too bad after all, but I was still very wary of these children. But when I went in the bedroom I got a big surprise. The girl and boy were curled up together on the bed. They both had teddies clutched to their chests. The girl went scarlet and thrust her teddy under the bedclothes in shame – but I saw. She was smaller than me, and had mousy hair that was meant to be in a ponytail, but the

ends were falling out. She looked strangely familiar. Then I twigged it.

She was in my class at my new school. She wasn't one of the bullies. She was one of the kids who also got teased a lot.

'I'm Milly. You know, I'm the new girl,' I said.

'I know,' she said timidly. 'I'm Moira. And this is Mick.'

She gave her brother a little nudge. He bent his head and mumbled. His T-shirt was on inside out and his socks didn't match. He looked the sort of kid who'd get teased too.

'What's this film then?' I said, sitting down on the bed with them.

It was an old old film called 'The Parent Trap.'

'Oh-oh,' I said. 'I've seen this. The parents get back together.'

'Yes,' said Moira. 'We've seen it before too. It's good.'

'Yes, it's good – but it's not really true,' I said. 'Parents hardly ever get back together after they split up. My mum and dad won't get back together and I don't expect yours will either.'

'I wish they would,' said Moira. Mick nodded again.

'Yeah, but wishes don't come true,' I said, feeling much older and wiser than them. 'But even if your mum and dad hate each other you have to remember they always love you. And you have to accept it if they go on to make new relationships.'

'Is your mum my dad's new relationship?' Moira asked, looking anxious.

I shrugged. 'Perhaps. They seem pretty keen on each other, don't they?

Moira and Mick nodded mournfully.

'But my mum's really nice. And your dad seems OK. So maybe it will work out all right.' I decided to change the subject. 'Do you two like chocolate cake?'

They nodded, this time with much more enthusiasm.

I got to cut the chocolate cake after we'd eaten

our roast chicken. I gave Moira and Mick a big slice each, every bit as big as mine.

Mum promised to let Moira and Mick help bake the next time she made a chocolate cake. She looked at me a little anxiously, as if I might object – but I just smiled.

I don't hate Moira and Mick. I quite like them. And maybe Moira and I can pal up in class. I think she could do with a good friend. I don't hate Michael either, though he's not a patch on my dad. I definitely don't hate Mum.

I don't hate Nan and Grandad either. They'd bought me a baby rabbit!

'I felt so mean because I knew you were missing that wretched gerbil,' said Nan.

'So I took her along to Pets at Home to see if we could find a replacement while you were at lunch,' said Grandad. 'She couldn't go near all the little mice and anything too rodenty – but once your nan saw this bunny she was really smitten.'

I love love love my little rabbit. She's got a new hutch out in the garden but I can take her out if I'm really careful. She burrowed down my sweatshirt just like Gilbert! I'm going to call her Happy.

Maybe it's going to be a Happy New Year after all.

✳ MAKE YOUR OWN ✳
CHRISTMAS TREE DECORATIONS!

Find some tracing paper, and trace around the bauble shapes on the next few pages – or, if you have a steady hand, see if you can simply copy them. Then cut them out carefully, and pop a little hole at the top to attach string so that you can hang your baubles up. Decorate each one with pictures of your favourite Jacqueline Wilson characters – there are lots of ideas here!

❋ MAKE YOUR OWN ❋
CHRISTMAS CARDS!

Find a plain piece of thin card or paper and fold it
in half down the middle – you may want to ask an
adult to help you with this. Then draw a reindeer
on the front of the card – here's a step-by-step
guide to show you how.

1. Draw the outline of the head and ears.

2. Add the antlers and a smiley face.

3. Pop some robins (or decorations) on the antlers, then colour in festive shades.

Fill the empty spaces around your design with
snowflakes, crackers, holly, Christmas puddings –
use the images on the opposite page for inspiration!

Here's an incredibly simple four-step way to draw a snowflake. They always have six sides or points and no two flakes are ever the same.

Mona lives with her aunty in a cottage on the
grand Somerset Estate. When a new member of the
family inherits the manor, Mona soon finds that
she cannot dance away from her past . . .

An unexpected gift leads to trouble for Hetty on
Christmas Day at the Foundling Hospital. Just when
all seems lost, a dear friend arrives to whisk her
away for a Christmas unlike any other . . .